A F

IN THE 100 YEARS that *Good Housekeeping* has been showcasing original fiction, no other author and no other story has elicited more abundant and positive reader response than LouAnn Gaeddert has with her moving tale *Perfect Strangers*.

We at St. Martin's Press are both proud and happy to bring you this wonderful story in paperback for the first time. We are proud to be the publisher of such an imaginative and sensitive author as LouAnn Gaeddert. And we are happy that you are about to discover how joyously rewarding a novel can be in the hands of an author as talented as she. Here, for your enjoyment, is the tale of two memorable people, Natalie and Jack, who will stay with you long after the book is done....

NATALIE

had finally achieved the success that was her ticket out of the city. Living in a beautiful old farmhouse complete with apple orchard, a new husband, and the hope of having a child, her dreams had finally come true. But she was living a lie...

JACK

was a stranger to her. Tall and secretive, he was a man of whom Natalie knew nothing ...except that he was willing to father the child Natalie ached to have.

PERFECT STRANGERS

PERFECT STRANGERS

LOUANN GAEDDERT

ST. MARTIN'S PRESS/NEW YORK

A condensed version of this novel appeared in the June, 1985 issue of *Good Housekeeping*.

PERFECT STRANGERS

Copyright © 1985, 1989 by LouAnn Gaeddert.

ISBN: 0-312-91545-4   Can. ISBN: 0-312-91546-2

Printed in the United States of America

First St. Martin's Press mass market edition/June 1989

10 9 8 7 6 5 4 3 2 1

SPRING

The twisted apple trees bloomed bravely in the blustery breeze of late May. He greeted them with a nod, and then, acting on impulse, turned his bicycle off the highway into the lane at the end of the orchard. He had not smiled for many weeks; he did not smile now, but his burden seemed lighter. He lowered his feet from the pedals and stood straddling his bike. Once again he nodded to the trees.

THE TREES BECKONED TO NATALIE JONES UNTIL SHE could ignore them no longer. She pulled a ragged sweater over her head, attached a piece

1

of textured paper to her easel and picked up her watercolors.

"By the shade of the old apple tree," she hummed as she began to paint. Silver, the cat, sunned herself on the porch of the little house which the orchard hid from the highway. Copper, the dog, sat beside the easel for a few moments and then went in search of rabbits. He returned to her side as the cyclist, whom Natalie neither saw nor heard, put his bike on the kickstand and stepped behind Natalie to look over her shoulder.

"Portrait of ancient brides," he whispered, startling her so that she dropped her brush. "Sorry," he said, leaning stiffly to pluck it from the grass.

"Wrong." She returned to her painting. "I call this 'Arthritic Soldiers in Full Dress.'"

She continued to paint, he to watch. Copper sniffed the stranger, curious but not alarmed.

"May I wander around your property, ma'am?" he asked after several minutes.

"Miss or Ms.," she replied automatically.

"Copper will go with you. If you have any questions, ask him."

Natalie completed her picture and sat back to admire it and her models. It was they who had drawn her to this spot two years ago, when she had decided to change her life.

On her thirty-second birthday she had asked herself a question she had asked many times: "Why am I living in this crowded white box?" For the first time, she had answered the question. "There is no valid reason to go on living like this."

True, her New York City apartment had seemed perfect once. Clean and modern with white walls, industrial shelving and boxy furniture. Over the years she had filled the shelves with books and the walls with prints. Nevertheless, her white apartment had come to remind her of a hospital operating room, sterile.

On that birthday morning, stumbling from the bedroom that doubled as a studio, she had passed the door with its three locks. No one should live barricaded behind three locks. In the tiny kitchen she had put her coffee on to brew and then stood in front of the living room window and looked down at the antlike creatures crawling along the street and then across to a terrace where five anemic evergreens stood in pots, the only green in view.

In the bathroom she had looked at herself in the mirror, something she seldom did. She knew that she looked like a brown mouse. Her straight hair, cut in a close cap, was brown. Her small eyes were a slightly darker brown. Even her skin had a sallow cast to it. Her features were plain.

She knew, too, that she had a mouselike personality. How many times had she met someone the day after a party they had both attended and been asked if she had been there? She had many acquaintances and few friends.

Was she self-pitying? Definitely not, for she was *Natalie* (no last name), an illustrator whose talent extended from delicate realistic pastels to abstract splashes of bold colors, from somber woodcuts to jolly collages. She had a large and adoring group of admirers who didn't care about her appearance and her personality. They were children, their parents, other adults—everyone interested in children's books. She was one of the youngest winners of the Caldecott Medal, which is presented annually by the American Library Association to the illustrator of the best picture book of the year.

She could select the manuscripts she wished to illustrate, and always had a backlog of work. Authors and editors were willing to wait for Natalie. Her income was adequate to her dreams.

At one time she had thought of her apartment as a way station along the road to a home she would share with some faceless man. On that birthday morning she had faced the painful facts: there would be no one sharing her life—which was no reason to deny herself the comforts of a home of her own.

That very day she had bought herself a birthday present, a small yellow car. The next day she headed north to the Berkshires, a range of green hills in Massachusetts that extends south into Connecticut and west into New York.

One week and several realtors later, she had met her soldiers who had seemed to escort her to the ancient little farmhouse with its peeling paint, and beyond to an energetic stream rushing through a miniature forest.

She was congratulating herself on her move—she loved this property even more now —when she heard the cracking of dry branches and the scrunch of dead leaves that announced the return of Copper and the cyclist. She turned toward them.

Although his bicycle was laden with camping equipment, it was hard to see this man as the outdoor type. He was much older than the average camper—forty, perhaps. His face, dominated by heavy black-rimmed glasses, was pasty white. His eyes, enlarged by thick lenses, were pale blue. His short straight hair was black. Moderately tall, narrow-shouldered. Wearing new jeans, a new wool shirt. She looked back at the bike. The sleeping bag was new, so was the bike. It did not take a Sherlock Holmes to recognize that this was no rugged athlete but a man who had spent months inside and was pedaling forth for what may have been the first time since his childhood.

"The dog said I'd have to ask you if I could camp here." He stood behind her, facing the easel. "The barn needs painting. Maybe I could do that for you."

"Had any experience painting?" The backs of his hands were white; she suspected that the palms were spotted with blisters.

"None. I expect you know how; you could teach me."

She shook her head, trying to think clearly. He stood silently, comparing her watercolor to the models. This man appreciated her orchard; that was something in his favor. (She was appalled by the number of cars that sped by on the highway, not slowing for the show of splendor.) Copper, a good judge of character, was accepting this stranger.

"Yes, I could teach you," she said at last. "You want to camp here? With a fire?" When he nodded, she paused again. "Not among my soldiers. Where?"

Silently they walked around her house,

through the woods behind it, to a small clearing beside the swollen stream.

"Here?" he said, pointing to a sandy stretch beside the stream.

She studied the surrounding trees and the tangle of bushes and weeds. "A very small fire? You'd watch it carefully? You'd . . ."

". . . I wouldn't burn your place down. That I assure you." He was scowling.

"Sorry to sound so fussy." She laughed. "I value these woods highly. I also value my shed and it needs painting. I'll get the paint this afternoon. You can set up your camp and start in the morning." She turned back toward the house. "Please ring your fire site with large stones," she called back over her shoulder.

Before she went to bed that night, Natalie stood in the back bedroom window looking out toward the stream. There was no blaze visible. What about that strange man? Why was he biking, camping out, offering to do work he had never done before? Why was his equipment all new? Suddenly she thought of prison; that would explain it. Still standing at the window she shook her head, bewildered. If anyone had asked her to describe the stereotypical prisoner, she would have used words like *crude* and *rough-spoken*. They did not fit her camper. Could he have been recently released from a mental institution? She shuddered.

"What do you think, Copper? Do you think he's okay?"

The dog licked her hand. Together they crept downstairs to check the locks on the windows and doors. *Why had she agreed to let a stranger camp on her land and paint her shed?* Maybe he'd have second thoughts and be gone in the morning; she hoped so.

Silver was already asleep on Natalie's bed. Copper lay down on the hooked rug with his back against the dust ruffle. Natalie lay stroking his velvety ear with one hand while she cuddled the cat in her other arm. Her animal friends were essential to her happiness.

During her first summer, she had rebuilt the house from the cellar up, new wiring, new plumbing, gallons of paint.

It was a simple house with a small, roofed

porch, a tiny entrance hall with narrow stairs opposite the door. The right half of the house was the living room with small-paned windows on three sides. Outside was the apple orchard. Inside were mellowed tables, a sofa, chairs and a worn oriental rug that had once graced her grandmother's house.

To the left of the hall was the dining room, which Natalie had converted into an all-white studio. It had a view of her mini-forest and contained utilitarian pieces from her New York City apartment. Behind the studio was the kitchen, about which there wasn't much to say except that it, too, had a view of the forest and a peek of the stream. Between the kitchen and the living room was another small hall and the back door.

Upstairs were two large bedrooms. A tiny bath had been squeezed in under the eaves with only an eyebrow window close to the floor for ventilation. Opposite the bathroom and over the front hall was another little room with one dormer window. She had had closets built in under the eaves of the front bedroom. She'd papered it herself with a calico print and had painted the woodwork. Then she had moved her grandmother's four-poster bed and cherry chests and hooked rugs into it. The other large bedroom contained plastic-clad furniture from her apartment. She seldom entered it except to check on her forest and her stream from the windows—as she had done this night.

She had had the house painted barn-red with white trim. Only the shed, which she used as a garage, stood as a reminder of the wreck the house had been.

At the end of that first summer Natalie had invited a favorite editor and an art director to spend Labor Day weekend with her. For the first time, she left her drawing board and her house projects to enjoy the pleasures of the Berkshires, the last production of a summer theater, the galleries, drives in the country.

Her house had seemed empty when her guests left. A series of thunder and lightning storms in October terrified her. The winter would be long and isolating. She needed a companion.

At the local animal shelter she had adopted a gray part-Angora kitten. Once she had the kitten in her arms, the wily attendant asked her to look at just one dog, a boxer not quite a year old but housebroken. His family had brought him to the shelter because they had been transferred out of the country. Since his arrival he had refused to eat. He was, the attendant said, starving and, as an act of kindness, would be put to sleep within the next day or two—unless, of course...Natalie had driven away from the shelter with a morose, aloof dog his former owners had named Copper, and a kitten she named Silver.

Silver had taken a quick tour of the house and had jumped onto a sunny wide windowsill in the studio to preen herself. Copper, who had been contented in the car, sniffed through the house, obviously searching for the beloved family that had deserted him, and then went to the door to scratch and whine.

Winning Copper's affection had taken most of the winter, but by spring he was tolerant of Silver and slobberingly devoted to Natalie. He was, in truth, her closest friend.

* * *

The cyclist was waiting beside the barn when she came out the next morning. She handed him a scraper and showed him how to use it. He gouged the old clapboard mercilessly; Natalie winced. He mumbled an apology and tried again. Just a scratch. A few more strokes and he had it.

Natalie turned back to the house. "By the way, my name is Natalie Jones."

"Jack," he said without looking up.

"Just Jack?"

Receiving no answer, she returned to the kitchen. "You go out there and keep an eye on him," she said to Copper. She opened the back door and watched while the big sleek dog ran around to the shed.

The man who had cycled into her lane was stiff; the man who came out of the woods on the second morning was even stiffer. Natalie stood in her kitchen window sipping coffee and watched him approach the shed. It was obvious that every muscle in his body screeched with pain.

She ran out to meet him. "Good morning, Jack," she called.

He nodded and went into the shed, returning with the ladder.

"You're stiff," she said. "You did too much yesterday. Why don't you take the day off? That shed has been waiting years for a coat of paint. It won't mind another day."

Responding not at all, Jack carefully placed the ladder against the wall and began to climb it. Was he deaf? His voice was normal. Still... She ran up to him and tapped his leg. He turned to look down at her and once again she suggested that he take the day off.

"I prefer not to take the day off." He continued his painful climb. When he could reach the eaves, he took the scraper out of his pocket and began to use it, competently.

The next day he was ready for primer. His first try with the roller and brush was a disaster. The paint rolled down his arms in sticky streaks. Once again he persevered until he had conquered the tools.

Gradually his body became more limber; his personality did not. He responded to her greetings in the morning with a nod. When she asked him where he was from, he ignored her question. When she commented that it was a beautiful day, he grunted. He was taciturn, even sullen, but he was a conscientious worker. She began to think of him as "the grouch."

One afternoon when he was high on the ladder, Natalie and Copper sneaked off to check his camp site. It was neat. The ashes from his fire were well contained by a circle of large rocks. He had built himself a shelter with a plastic tarp supported by a low-hanging branch and other branches stuck into the ground. He had a lantern and a skillet and little else that was visible. She and Copper walked back to the road several hundred feet from their lane so that their tenant would not suspect that they had been spying on him.

"Satisfied?" Jack sneered from the top of the ladder as they approached the shed.

Natalie had no idea how he spent his evenings. He walked off the job about six and was back at it again by eight the next morning. At noon he disappeared into the woods for an hour. His determined distance aroused her curiosity. He may or may not have been a convict or a mental patient. He was definitely an enigma.

The shed was beginning to look like a mate to the house, at least from one side where the clapboard had received its final coat of red and the trim around the tiny window had been painted white. After Jack had left for the day, Natalie walked all the way around it, admiring his work. It was a better job than professional painters had done on her house. Most people would consider it too good for a shed. Not Natalie; she would rather pay for the extra hours it took to do a first-rate job than to save money on a sloppy one. She had tried to pay Jack at the end of his first week. He had insisted on waiting until he had finished the job.

From far off came a clap of thunder, and Natalie and Copper retreated to the house and ate their dinners. The radio began to stutter as darkness fell. Natalie turned it off. All of a sudden the sky lit up like noon. She stifled a scream, shoved the leftovers into the refrigerator and ran out of the kitchen with its flashing windows. She locked the back door and pulled the heavy drapes over the living room windows. Then she unplugged the television, picked up a book and curled up in a big wingback chair with Silver in her arms, Copper resting his nose on one of her feet.

Her fear was irrational, which made it no less real. As a child she had hidden from the flash of lightning and the crash of thunder by pulling the blankets up over her head. As an adult she hid behind a small cat and a large dog. Rain pounded on the roof. The wind howled. She buried her face in Silver's fur and trembled. Copper licked her ankle.

There was a bang at the back door. Copper began to howl. A clap of thunder. Such a racket, Natalie laughed weakly. The banging continued.

"Dammit. Let me in."

Jack! She hadn't even thought of him out there under his flimsy plastic. Ashamed, she dumped Silver from her lap and ran to throw open the back door. He stumbled into the kitchen and stood there streaming. His shirt and jeans clung to his body; his hair was plastered to his head. She handed him a wad of paper towels and then watched, amazed, as he ignored the glasses through which he could scarcely see and carefully wiped every drop from a black leather case.

Natalie ran upstairs and picked up a stack of towels and the pink-terry cloth robe that hung on the back of the bathroom door. The kitchen flashed bright as day as she dropped the robe and towels on the kitchen table and retreated to the living room before the drumroll.

She was again huddled in her chair, clutching her cat, when Jack appeared before her. He turned around silently, modeling the too-small pink robe. She laughed at his knobby knees, hairy legs and bare feet beneath the robe. He smiled; she'd never seen him smile before. The smile faded and he went back to the kitchen. Between claps of thunder, she could hear his footsteps and the banging of cupboard doors. Then the welcome smell of coffee.

"I'm lacing it with your brandy," he shouted to her. "Cream and sugar?"

"Black, please. And thank you."

He returned with two mugs of coffee in his

hands and a gleaming flute under his arm. So that's what had been in the carefully tended black case.

Setting the mugs on the coffee table, he sat down cross-legged on the floor. "Want me to play?"

Natalie nodded and began to relax as he played a theme from *The Four Seasons*. He played on and on, stopping only to sip his coffee. The thunder receded. The cat and the dog napped. At last Natalie picked up their mugs and returned to the kitchen to refill them. His clothes were laid out on chairs to dry, newspapers protecting the floor from drips. Her dinner dishes were stacked neatly in the sink. She refilled the mugs, took them back to the living room and tried to thank Jack for his music.

"You're afraid of thunder," he said matter-of-factly.

She nodded. "And lightning. Your music was a tonic. But should you be using your hands to paint my shed? You must have blisters. A professional musician must surely..."

"I'm not professional. You show me your work now." It was a command.

Natalie selected a half dozen picture books from the shelves in her studio and brought them to him. Most adults, with no special interest in children's books, would leaf through them quickly, say something absurd like "charming" and put them aside. Not Jack; he read every word. He examined every picture. He grinned and pointed to a baby rabbit peering out of a hole in the background of one picture. It was a detail that her editor had not seen until the book was printed. She had thought of Jack as expressionless. That was before she had watched him play his flute and read her books. She began to sketch him.

When he had finished the last book, he stacked all six of them neatly on the coffee table. Then he stood behind her and looked at her sketch. She turned quickly to see if she had insulted the grouch with her silly picture of him in a woman's robe, reading a Mother Goose. He laughed aloud, another first. Then he turned serious.

"Kids who get your books are lucky," he said. "I never read a children's book like that before."

"What do you mean? Of course you never read one of mine before. I didn't begin to produce them until twelve years ago. The second from the bottom was my first book. Surely you read books similar to them when you were a child. Your *Mother Goose* must have had most of the same words that mine has; yours just had a larger format."

"I never read *Mother Goose*. Made me feel pretty stupid when I started school. All the other kids knew that Humpty Dumpty was an egg. Not I."

Not to know that—or that Little Miss Muffet sat on a tuffet, or that Jack Sprat could eat no fat—seemed impossible to Natalie. "Storybooks? Someone must have read to you. Maybe one of Marjorie Flack's *Angus* books? Or *Peter Rabbit*?"

"No. Not until I started school. I must have had an ABC and some kind of a counting book. My mother would have considered them educational. She believed in reading to learn, not for entertainment. Tonight I've discovered what I missed. Thank you."

"You've never had children of your own?"

"Never had a wife." He got up and headed for the kitchen.

"Where are you going?" she asked.

"It's stopped raining but the ground will be wet. Thought maybe I could sleep in your shed."

"I have an extra room, with an honest-to-goodness bed. Think you could readjust to a mattress? It's fairly hard."

He searched her face and she found herself wishing she were pretty. Then he shrugged. "You're sure you won't be afraid. You needn't be."

More's the pity, she thought as she picked up Silver and nudged Copper awake and to the back door. She directed Jack to the back bedroom and he went on up while she waited for Copper.

Although it was almost three when she climbed into bed, she lay awake for a long time. Could Jack be the man she was looking for?

Natalie had been perfectly content in her house with Copper and Silver until the second spring, when she had received a call from an advertising agency that led to a commission to do a series of pictures of babies for a baby food campaign. She painted a Chinese baby, a black baby and a pair of blond twins.

"What would you think of adopting a child?" she had asked Copper one night. "It won't be easy since I'm single, but we might get a minority baby, or an older child or a handicapped child."

Copper expressed his approval by licking her hand. Silver jumped into her lap and preened herself.

"I'm not asking you, Silver. I know what you think on the subject. You think you are all I could possibly need."

Silver purred loudly.

"I hear you. But purr and meow are all you say. I'm going to think about adoption whether you like it or not. I could give a child love and a good home, everything it could need—except a father."

Natalie did think about adoption. Then one day in the general store she had spotted an infant sleeping in a sling on his mother's breast.

She told the mother about her baby project and asked if she could paint this newborn.

Two days later she was driving into a rutty driveway toward an unfinished log house. The woman, whose name was Babs, ushered her into the kitchen and apologized briefly for the mess (the appliances were in place, but the cabinets were only roughed in and were supplemented by boxes that held the dishes and food). A little boy about three came through a curtained doorway and hid behind his mother. The baby was sleeping in a basket. Babs poured coffee into mugs and cleared a space at the kitchen table.

They had chatted briefly about themselves. Babs' husband was a teacher in the Stockbridge school. They had two other children, in school now, and they were building their house themselves.

"We thought we could get it all done during summer vacation last year, but everything just took longer than we had thought and we ran out of money and..." She shrugged her shoulders. "Oh, well, it will all be done one day, maybe during this summer vacation, God willing."

The baby woke and cried and Babs lifted her sweatshirt and scooped him to her breast. Then she sat in a big rocking chair and stroked his downy head while he nursed. Natalie stared as Babs' features seemed to be transformed. Natalie had seen her as a plain woman with freckles scattered across her squashed nose and round cheeks. Her black hair was drawn into one thick braid that reached almost to her slightly pudgy waist. But while she nursed her baby she seemed classically beautiful. Her wide mouth turned up slightly at the corners. Her eyes were soft and tender. Natalie pulled a pencil and pad from her purse and began to sketch the modern madonna. Later she sketched the baby for one of the ads.

When she returned home, Natalie went straight to her studio to paint the madonna in oils. She would title it "Contentment." As she painted, tears began to trickle down her cheeks. She blew her nose on her paint rag as she imagined what it must be to carry a baby, give birth to it, nurse it. Babs knew. She had experienced it four times. While she, Natalie . . . not even once.

The next week she had gone to New York to deliver her baby paintings to the agency. She also went to see a doctor, who examined her and said she was perfectly healthy and that he would arrange for her to be artificially inseminated if that was her choice. He assured her that the father would be bright, probably a medical student, and healthy. He gave her statistics about how many artificial inseminations took place each year.

He refused, however, to arrange the procedure for her until she had thought about it for several months. "This is not like choosing a pair of shoes," he said. "The result will be a life that will demand years of nurture. Imagine the child growing up, the questions it will ask, how you will answer. Imagine the child sick, naughty, defiant."

Natalie went home and did just that. It was the questions the child might ask that made her uncomfortable. She could not find answers that were both satisfying and truthful. She tried to forget the idea, reminding herself that she had a career, home and animals she loved. She was a lucky woman; she didn't need a baby. She almost convinced herself, but not quite.

She couldn't stop fantasizing: a wedding, a honeymoon, a scrapbook filled with photographs a child could pour over. A pregnancy and then a divorce. Many children these days had divorced parents. Some never saw their fathers. She'd done the jacket for a novel about mail-order brides once; she'd never heard of mail-order husbands. Still, someplace there might be someone who would go through the picture-producing ritual, impregnate her, and leave her—for money.

She could afford to pay. In addition to her royalties and fees, she had a small inheritance from her grandmother. Her father had invested it well. Somewhere there had to be a man so desperate for money that...

She had bought a copy of *New York* magazine and read the classifieds: "Bright young lawyer interested in opera and scuba diving seeks tall, beautiful woman for candlelight dinners, trips to romantic islands, etc."

She composed an ad of her own: "Homely

professional woman seeks intelligent, healthy man to marry her, father baby and disappear. Willing to pay top price." She read the ad to Copper, laughed and tore it up.

When the babies were painted, she had tackled the small yard around her house. She seeded the lawn, had a man come with a Roto-tiller to prepare a small vegetable garden, planted impatiens around the foundation of her house and hung a huge basket of begonias beside her front door.

By midsummer her house was blooming and manicured. Only the shed remained an eyesore. She'd paint it herself when she had time. In the meantime, she had a backlog of work waiting in her studio which she worked on seven days a week. She was busy and happy.

Still, babies had forced themselves into her dreams. Whenever she met a man, and she met few, she could not help asking herself if he could be a father to the child she longed to bear and to nurse. There had been a recently divorced electrician who had worked on her house; he was loud and crude and she could not imagine letting him touch her. There was a dear young man in his early twenties who worked at the local hardware store. She had heard that many people considered older women to be good educators of young men. Natalie was a virgin; no doubt less experienced than he.

Now Natalie was thirty-four and a stranger named Jack was sleeping in the bedroom across the hall. Was he the partner she was seeking? She knew nothing about him. What would be his contribution to the gene pool? Not beauty. But musical talent. How about brains? How could one tell? He certainly spoke—when he spoke—like an intelligent person. Was he unstable, insane, criminal?

She awoke with a start, checked her clock and saw that it was almost eleven. Copper was gone from his sleeping place on the hooked rug. Silver nuzzled her neck. She sniffed—coffee— and smiled as she thought about the night before.

Then she got up and dressed in her usual

jeans and a new red turtleneck. Red was a good color for her. In the bathroom she applied lipstick and a trace of blusher. *Silly girl*, she said to herself.

The living room drapes had been opened so that sunshine streamed into the room. The light on the electric pot glowed, and she poured herself a mug of coffee and looked around the room. There was no trace of Jack except for the flute case sitting on the floor beside the back door.

She took her coffee outside and shouted "Good morning" to Jack, who was at the top of the ladder. He nodded in response. "How were things out at your camp?" she asked.

"Soggy."

"So why don't you pack everything into my car and I'll drive you to the laundromat in town? I can't think of any other way that your sleeping bag will get dry by nighttime."

"Want to finish this side. Maybe this afternoon." He continued to spread red paint on the clapboard.

So much for her new shirt and the blusher,

Natalie thought ruefully. "Did you have break-fast?"

"Yes."

"Thanks for playing your flute for me last night and for making the coffee this morning."

He didn't respond and she turned and went back to the house. She made herself a piece of toast and drove off to town.

Late that afternoon she went back to the shed and put her car keys beside the paint can where Jack was working. "I've already done my shopping. You can take my car if you want to go to the laundromat."

"Thanks." He paused. "For everything."

He worked until five. Then she watched from the house while he loaded the trunk of her car and drove off. She'd probably never see her car again. So be it. She'd have the most expensively painted shed in the country and she'd know something about this man. But he would return. She knew that as soon as she went to the kitchen. His flute was still there. She knew almost nothing about this man except this: he would never go off without his flute. And, of course, he didn't.

* * *

The next day Natalie started work on what would be a lavishly illustrated *Child's Garden of Verses*. She'd been reading Stevenson's poems all spring. She began with one called "Summer Sun":

> *Though closer still the blinds we pull*
> *To keep the shady parlor cool,*
> *Yet he will find a chink or two*
> *To slip his golden fingers through. . . .*

The setting would be her parlor; the characters, her pets.

Silver was happy to pose. All that was required of her was to curl up in the big chair and sleep; she was good at that. Copper wanted to romp outside, not pose.

"Look here, Copper. I don't ask much of you. Remember, I rescued you from the shelter. I feed you. I've given you twenty acres of land to explore. All I ask is a few minutes of your precious time to sit and look handsome." She spoke crossly, but Copper responded by jumping up on her and licking her face.

"If you love me so much, why don't you prove it by doing this one thing for me? Sit."

He sat, looking up into her face, and she began to try to capture his expectant expression. "Good dog," she said at last. "I'll work from this sketch. You can go play now." She opened the door for him and he ran out like a six-year-old after a day in school.

The next day she called Babs and asked to borrow Bobby, the three-year-old, now four, who had once hidden behind his mother in the half-finished kitchen, now finished. He followed her eagerly to the stream. She made a fleet of bark ships with leaf sails. She launched the first one, then sat back to sketch. Bobby was an impish, freckle-faced blond and he squatted beside the water with his little bottom dangling in the air above his pudgy legs. He concentrated on his "boats" while she captured the rapt expression on his face.

Dark brown is the river,
Golden is the sand.

It flows along forever,
With trees on either hand.

Green leaves a-floating,
Castles on the foam,
Boats of mine a-boating—
Where will all come home?

On goes the river
And out past the mill,
Away down the valley,
Away down the hill.

Away down the river,
A hundred miles or more,
Other little children
Shall bring my boats ashore.

When she had completed her sketch, she sat back against the trunk of a tree and contemplated the child. Her heart was filled with longing, her arms ached to hold him.

Suddenly he jumped up and ran along the stream to capture a boat that was heading out to sea. Then he stopped.

"What's that?" he asked, pointing to Jack's reconstructed shelter.

Without waiting for an answer he climbed under a flap and was sitting cross-legged on Jack's sleeping bag when Natalie arrived to pull him out.

"This is Jack's house," she said. "We're trespassing—that means we don't belong here. Come on out." She tugged on his leg and looked around curiously. There was the bike. Next to it was a box. The flute case, wrapped in several layers of plastic, lay on top of the box. Inside the box were books—*The Scarlet Letter*, in paperback, a copy of her *Mother Goose*! . . .

Natalie grabbed Bobby and retreated quickly; she had no right to invade this man's privacy. She pulled the child along as she raced back to her house, where she looked down into the little boy's startled eyes.

"Sorry," she said. "Let's go have some sandwiches. Peanut butter? I'll read to you while we eat."

He grinned at her and she took him in her arms and held him close, cherishing the warmth of his little body next to hers.

* * *

That night Natalie sat on her front stoop after dinner. Darkness fell and she was still sitting there. She wanted to think logically; instead she dreamed. The movie in her mind was of herself with a baby at her breast patting her face. She saw the child taking its first steps and herself standing at the end of the lane with the child waiting for the school bus. She saw them curled together in her big bed reading Beverly Cleary's funny books. She forced herself to look at the movie of the teenage child staying out late and defying her. Again and again she replayed the reel of the nursing baby.

It was easy to dream about bearing and raising a child. It was almost impossible to think logically about how that might be accomplished. Was Jack a possible father? He was the only likely candidate she had met since she first began thinking about motherhood. She could not realistically expect to meet that many more candidates in the time left for her to safely bear a child. As the pop psychologists phrased it, her clock was running out.

But she knew nothing about Jack, not even his last name. She knew only that he was no beauty. Any child they would produce together would have little chance of physical attractiveness—unless, of course, it took after her sister.

Veronica was lovely. A natural blonde with a long slim body, large blue eyes, a small tilted nose. *You are Veronica's sister?* How many tactless people had asked that question? It was one of the reasons Natalie had left Ohio so many years ago.

It was not only Veronica's beauty. Their parents, especially their mother, were proud of her. Veronica had "married well"—an ambitious young doctor. (Natalie thought he was a stick with no sense of humor, but she had never heard anyone share her opinion.) Veronica lived in a "lovely" fake colonial house. She had two children, a boy first and then a girl, of course. She kept her house beautifully. (The children had to take their shoes off at the door and they weren't allowed to make messes. When Natalie visited, she delighted in introducing them to finger paints and clay, in the basement.) Veronica served on important committees and played a solid game of tennis. She was a totally satisfactory daughter, unlike Natalie.

Her poor parents had never understood Natalie's move to New York. They were even more baffled by her decision to buy a house in Massachusetts, the home of the witch-hunts and the Kennedys. A single girl should live near her parents, her mother said. Her father agreed. *Out, damn thoughts*, Natalie said to herself. *On with the business at hand.*

What about Jack's intelligence? His character? She knew nothing of either. He played the flute and he had bought a copy of *Mother Goose*. He worked diligently. These were all pluses. He was a grouch. He might be violent, for all she knew. She could not discard the idea that he might have served time in prison—or a mental institution.

Suddenly she found herself laughing aloud. *What do you expect, old girl? A fine old family, an IQ of 140, a degree from Yale, honesty, beauty. Forget it! A man with all those qualities could not be bought for any amount of money!*

Could Jack be bought? That was the question. Natalie spent the night flailing around in her bed and awoke in a pool of sweat.

Jack was working on the front of the shed when Natalie approached him after a morning spent pacing from her studio through the living room and back again.

"Looks like you'll be finished tomorrow if the weather holds," she said. "I expect you'll be anxious to get on your way."

He nodded.

"How about coming to dinner tonight? We'll celebrate a job well done. Seven?"

Again he nodded.

Natalie spent the rest of the day shopping and cooking. Then she ran upstairs to bathe and dress. Nothing too fancy, she decided, and pulled a navy turtleneck with red ladybugs over her head and tucked it into a jeans skirt. She slipped her feet into sandals with just enough heel to set off her legs. She'd been told that she had good legs. Then she made up her face lightly but with great care.

On the dot of seven he appeared at her

back door in fresh jeans and a navy-and-green-striped polo shirt. He smiled at her and she suddenly thought that he really wasn't all that homely. They discussed the shed while they sipped wine before dinner. Or, to be more accurate, *she* discussed the shed.

She had set the gateleg table in the living room with straw place mats and cotton batik napkins. She brought on a dinner of roast beef, baked potatoes and spinach salad. He held her chair for her; he'd picked up good manners somewhere. While they ate she tried to draw him into conversation.

"You play the flute so very well. Where did you study?"

"Boston."

"You must have studied for many years. Did you ever play professionally?"

"No."

So much for that topic. "Do you think there is a solution for the problems in the Near East?"

"No."

So much for that. "Did you live in Boston long?"

"Yes. This is a good dinner. Do you *like* to

cook or do you just do everything well?" He was, finally, making some effort to converse.

"I do like to cook and I don't do everything well. I can't sing or even play 'Chopsticks' on the piano. Do you like to cook and do you do everything well? You certainly have become a good painter."

"I've never done much cooking and I do almost nothing well...anymore." There was bitterness in his voice.

They finished their dinner in silence. As she was clearing the table and bringing on the coffee and sherbet, she tried to put her thoughts in order. How could she ask this man to marry her? It was impossible.

He stood when she returned to the table. She saw that he had poured them each another glass of wine. He took a long swallow of his and then turned to look straight at her. "Why did you invite me to dinner?" Each word was embedded in an ice cube.

She could not look at him and hung her head.

"If you were merely being social—or rewarding a faithful employee for a job well done

—you would not be so nervous. You were frightened of the storm but you weren't like this."

"Like what?"

"Up and down. Talking nonstop. Look at your napkin."

Her napkin was a crushed, sweaty ball.

"Now, look at me," he commanded. "Tell me why you invited me to dinner."

How dare he command her! She looked straight at him and hoped he could see the fire in her heart. "Because I want a baby," she said slowly and very clearly.

"Because you want a baby?" The question started as a shout and ended as a whisper. "I'm not a medical doctor."

"I didn't think you were."

"So why . . . ?"

"Because one of the things I don't do well is thinking. I want a baby and I'm looking for a temporary husband to father that baby. I thought you might be a likely candidate. Obviously you're not interested, so please leave. You can take your coffee with you."

He sat staring at her. "You don't need a husband to have a baby. You must know that."

"I do. But I don't want my child ever to hear the word 'bastard.' Divorce is common these days. A child could understand that and hold up his head."

"So what's the deal?" Jack chuckled.

She bristled. "It's not amusing. At least not to me."

"I see that," he said seriously. "What did you have in mind?"

She tried to sip her coffee and choked. He got up and banged her on the back. At last she stopped coughing.

"Now, answer my question. What did you have in mind?"

"I want someone who will marry me properly with a minister, a honeymoon and a scrapbook the child could examine when he got older. I want that person to live with me for an agreed-upon length of time, probably six months—or until I am pregnant. Then he can go away and I will file for divorce. I am willing to pay for the service."

"Willing to pay? A stud fee? Why should you have to buy a husband?" He waited for an answer but received none. "Drink your coffee."

She drank, anxious to demonstrate that this was a simple business deal, nothing more. The coffee tasted like medicine. Then she ate her sherbet. In the meantime, he went to the kitchen and came back with the coffeepot and refilled their cups.

"Okay, I'm willing." His face was a blank.

Natalie panicked. "But I don't know anything about you. Are you bright? Do you have any diseases that could be inherited?"

"You should have thought of that before you asked me. I do have poor eyesight. Does that disqualify me? What about you? I know you're bright, and talented. I watched you with the kid you were sketching yesterday. I expect you'd be a good mother. You don't wear glasses and you have lovely teeth. What else should I know about the mother of my child? I don't want to be responsible for a genetic misfit any more than you do."

The tables had turned; he was questioning her. She was speechless.

"So when do we get married?" he asked at last. "I don't suppose you want to try for the pregnancy and then get married."

"No. Go back to your camp. Think about it. If

you're still willing in the morning, we'll talk about it. If you change your mind, you can just leave. I can finish the shed." She went to her studio and returned with her checkbook and a calculator. "You've worked how many hours at . . . ?"

"Stop. We've done enough business for one night."

"But you may want to leave in the morning."

"I'll leave a forwarding address." He chuckled again, lifted her chin and kissed her lightly on the lips. "Good night, fiancée."

At the door he turned. "Just to ease your mind, I have an IQ of 154. Too bad I got it by brain transplant. My original IQ was 67." He was still laughing as he crossed the lawn toward his camp.

Natalie was laughing, too. So he did have both brains and a sense of humor. She cleaned up the kitchen and went to bed, laughing with satisfaction.

The sky was turning from black to gray when Natalie awoke and stretched contentedly.

She lay on her back, staring at the ceiling and remembering the events of the night before. Jack—she still didn't know his last name—had agreed to try to father a child with her. She began to wonder why. Apprehension swallowed her contentment. Could any sane man fall in with such a harebrained scheme? Perhaps he was desperate for money, but he hadn't asked how much she would pay. How much would she pay? She hadn't considered that.

She tried to laugh at herself, but her laugh turned into a sob and she rolled herself into a ball around Silver, who licked her cheek and purred.

Why think about money? Jack had surely come to his senses; he was probably just waiting for her to pay him for painting the shed so he could pedal on. Should she go downstairs to make him a cup of coffee before he left? To show him there were no hard feelings, that she, too, in the cool light of the early morning had come to her senses? But she hadn't. She still wanted a baby and she knew that she would never again be able to approach any man with her absurd scheme.

So she lay in her grandmother's four-poster, where many children had been conceived, waiting for the morning. The minutes crawled by in slow motion, the hours.

Copper was demanding to be released. Natalie looked at the clock—nine—and threw her robe around her—the same one Jack had worn the night of the storm. When she opened the back door, Copper ran out, barking.

"Morning, Copper."

"What are you doing?" Natalie found herself staring at him.

"Painting the shed." He turned away, disgusted. "I knew you'd change your mind."

"Not I. But surely you?" she whispered.

"I agreed, didn't I? You get dressed and put on the coffeepot while I finish up here."

"You're very bossy."

" 'Wives obey your husbands.' That's what Saint Paul said. You might just as well get in practice." He strode back to the shed.

A half an hour later he walked into her kitchen, took her in his arms and kissed her firmly.

"What's your name?" she asked.

He laughed heartily. "Allow me to introduce myself. My name is John V. Berkhardt. Just call me Jack the Stud." All traces of humor disappeared. "When does this charade begin?"

The words *mental institution* popped into her head. This man was entirely too volatile. One minute he was making jokes, the next he was sullen and bitter. She poured out two mugs of coffee with shaking hands.

"There's still time to back out," he said, as if reading her thoughts.

"It's just that I know so little about you," she whispered.

"Look, lady, this was your idea, not mine. If you're worried that I'm a criminal or mentally or physically ill, forget it. There are reasons, which I never intend to reveal to you, why your proposal is attractive to me. Now I'm going back to my painting. I should be finished by noon. If you want to continue this discussion, come on out. If not..." He let the screen door slam behind him.

It *was* her idea. At her desk she studied a calendar and then wrote out a check on her money fund. She put the check on the kitchen table along with a pile of notes and lists. Then she made roast beef sandwiches and went outside.

The crosspieces on the shed door were gleaming white and Jack was cleaning his brushes.

"You've done a wonderful job, Jack. Thank you. How many hours have you worked?"

"Didn't keep track."

"Then I'll make an estimate. How much an hour?"

"So you don't want to go ahead with the wedding? I knew you'd change your mind." There was bitterness in his voice.

"No, I haven't. I want to go ahead with the six-month marriage. Painting the shed is separate..."

"Why? They're both jobs. Painting a shed, fathering a child. Just services you can buy..."

She didn't know how to react to this bitter man. What, if anything, to say. "I've made us some sandwiches. If you'll come in when you're finished..."

He nodded.

Natalie did the talking while they ate at the

kitchen table. She spelled out the schedule she had in mind in the same methodical manner she used when discussing a contract with an editor. He objected to nothing but insisted on planning the honeymoon. He accepted her check for ten thousand dollars with which he would pay for the groom's part of the wedding and the honeymoon. At the end of six months she would give him another ten thousand dollars.

"What if you're not pregnant?"

"I will be very sad, but my body will know more of its capabilities—and its limitations."

Once again she mentioned the shed and opened her checkbook to pay him for painting it.

"Stop it," he shouted as he reached across the table and closed the checkbook. "What kind of a man...? Sorry, I've adequately demonstrated what kind of a man I am. Just don't try to give me any more money today." He waved the check for ten thousand dollars in her face. "*This* is almost more than my pride can accept. Now, tell me the details of this charade. What church?"

Jack said he had no religious faith; she suggested a Protestant service at home.

That afternoon they went to see the minister of the local church. He looked like a teenager and must have felt like one, because he offered to counsel them and then seemed immensely relieved when Jack said they were old enough to know what they were doing.

The next stop was for blood tests and then the jewelry store in Pittsfield, where they selected one wide gold band which they left to be engraved.

Without consulting her, Jack, who was driving her car, pulled into a parking lot beside a flossy restaurant on the Lenox road. While they were eating, a photographer stopped at the table. Natalie demurred. Jack insisted. He scooted his chair around close to hers, put his arm around her and gazed deep into her eyes.

"For the scrapbook," he explained when the photographer had finished. "This, too." He handed her an envelope. Inside was a pressed sprig of apple blossoms. "Anything else?" he asked.

"The ordeal." She sighed. "We've got to phone my parents."

They had already agreed that it would be a

small wedding. No one but immediate family. Jack said he had no immediate family, so the only guests would be her parents and her sister and brother-in-law and their children.

"And they are going to ask all kinds of embarrassing questions. Number one will be, what do I do? Tell them I'm a teacher who has just left one position and is looking for another."

"Where were you?"

"Eastern Massachusetts, a suburb of Boston."

"What do you teach?"

"Math."

"Where did you go to college?"

He paused. "Tell them a university in Massachusetts and slur so they'll hear it as the University of Massachusetts."

"You're not going to tell me, either."

"No. But I did go to college, if that matters to you."

"I don't think that it does. It's the IQ that counts and you say that you attained genius status via brain transplant..." They laughed together.

While Jack was putting the car in the shed,

Natalie dialed her parents' number. Jack entered the studio in time to hear most of her side of the conversation.

"The last Saturday of the month... Yes, I mean June... I know it's soon, but we just can't wait..." She giggled into the phone coyly while grimacing at Jack. "Mother! No, I do not *have* to get married. I *want* to get married... What?... Nice-looking, not a glamour boy... He's a teacher... Math... How old is he?" She turned to him and then back to the phone. "He's thirty-eight... No, he's never been married... I don't know why... Mother! He says he has never been married and I believe him... Stop it, Mother... I believe him... No, I haven't known him very long... He's been painting my shed... Yes, he's very handy." She stifled a giggle. "He plays the flute, too... Sure, Dad. You can talk with him. I'll put him on." She handed the phone to Jack.

"Thank you... I'll cherish her, too..." Jack said into the mouthpiece. "Yes, I love her madly. She's..."

Natalie grabbed the phone from him. "It's me again. No, Mother, I haven't decided what

I'll wear . . . No, Mother, you don't need to come right away . . . Yes, Mother, I think I can make all the arrangements by myself . . . Come on the twenty-sixth."

Natalie picked up a ballpoint pen from her desk and began to tap it on the mouthpiece of the phone, interrupting her mother's harangue. Then she shouted into the mouthpiece. "There's some disturbance on the line. I can't hear you. Sorry, Mother, I'll phone again tomorrow night . . . Yes, Dad, I'll phone tomorrow."

She hung up, feeling limp. "It isn't fair to put you through this." She sighed. "Shall we elope?"

"What about the scrapbook? I think that's important—for the child."

"You were terrific with my father. Thank you."

He turned to the door, letting it slam behind him.

The next morning he moved his bicycle and his camping gear into the shed and asked her to drive him to the bus in Stockbridge. He had things to do before the wedding. What things, she did not know. She did not ask.

When the bus appeared rumbling down the highway toward them, he got out of the car and then turned back to lean into the window. "Don't worry that I won't come back. I'll be here on the day before the wedding. I've made a reservation at the Berkshire Inn. I'll take your family to dinner there that night. Groom's dinner, or some such. I'll also bring a camera so we can get lots of pictures. Till then . . ." He kissed her lightly and boarded the bus.

Would he return? He said he would.

Two days later Natalie went to New York to discuss the Stevenson book with her publisher —and to buy a wedding dress. She was so sallow that she could not wear white or ivory. She looked best in strong colors, but one just could not get married in red or kelly green. When, in despair, she had decided that there was not a suitable dress in all of New York City, she found it. It was blue silk with a full skirt beneath a nipped-in waist and tiny self ruffles at the high neck and at the cuffs of the long full sleeves. She bought lingerie, several shirts, skirts and pants, a blazer and a cotton dress, almost a complete new wardrobe.

Finally she selected a wedding present for Jack. She didn't know if he was a man who had everything or nothing. She bought him a silver pen-and-pencil set, dull but safe.

All this took three days, during which time Silver and Copper had been cared for by a neighbor boy who came in every morning and evening. The animals made certain that she understood that they had been miserable in her absence. Copper jumped all over her, licked her face and slobbered in wild enthusiasm. Silver took one look at her, lifted her nose disdainfully and walked away. She refused to come in for dinner. She snubbed Natalie until bedtime, when she graciously forgave all and jumped up on the bed and snuggled, purring, against her shoulder.

The next day the United Parcel man delivered a large box, no return address. Inside was a deluxe scrapbook, white leather cover and plastic-encased pages. No card. It was beautiful. Jack was coming back for the wedding!

In the mail the next day she received a large manila envelope with no return address. Inside were four sheets of paper. The first was handwritten:

Enclosed is a love letter for the scrapbook. I did my best to sound like a lovesick Romeo. Hope it fills the bill. Also enclosed is a letter of agreement. As you see, I have signed both copies. Please consider, make necessary changes, and sign so that I may have a copy for my files before the wedding. This is, after all, a business deal. I had planned to have this agreement drawn by a lawyer but found it impossible to explain the situation to a third party. Therefore, I wrote this myself but expect it to be legally binding should we have problems in the future.

The second sheet was also handwritten:

Darling little Natalie,
Only ten days and you will be my own. They seem like ten years, so great is my longing for you. I never before knew what love was lying latent in my breast. And to think that my love is returned by one so lovely, so talented as you! Thank you, my dearest, for present and future joy.

All my love, Jack

She thrust the letter between the leaves of the new scrapbook. Beautiful words! She wondered if he had composed them or copied them.

She turned quickly to the two typewritten sheets, one of which was a copy:

Agreement
Between
Natalie Elizabeth Jones and John V. Berkhardt

We, the undersigned, being of age and of sound mind, have willingly agreed to a marriage of no more than six months, the purpose of which is to conceive a child. John V. Berkhardt will leave the home of Miss Natalie Jones whenever conception has been confirmed by medical tests or at the end of six months whether or not conception has taken place. If there is a child, he or she will be the sole responsibility of the mother, physically, mentally, morally and financially.

Although the father promises not to interfere with the child's upbringing in any way, he reserves the right to visit the child twice a year, each visit to be limited to three hours. These visits will be arranged at the convenience of the mother and take place in her home if she so requests. These visits may continue until the child reaches the age of eighteen. The mother will be obliged to inform the father of any major crises in the child's life.

In the interest of the child's mental health, each parent will present the other in a positive light. There will be no criticism or complaints against the other in the child's presence.

Jack had signed and dated the odious document and left a line for her to sign and date. She did as requested. Then she shoved the two agreements back into the envelope, and wept.

She felt dirty. She had read a Thomas Hardy novel about a man who had sold his wife and child. Was she better? She was buying a child . . . or trying to buy a child. She took a bath and still she felt dirty. She continued to weep, all the rest of the afternoon and far into the night.

The following week Natalie's mother drove into her lane in a car she had rented at the Albany airport.

"I just couldn't wait, darling, to meet your young man," she cooed as she skipped into the house. Natalie's mother was sixty going on sixteen.

"He's out of town and won't be back until the day before the wedding." Natalie tried to smile.

"Where did he go?"

"Boston." Natalie could hardly say she didn't know.

"Do you hear from him every day?"

"He sent this scrapbook. Just one letter. I've been in New York selecting my trousseau."

That diverted Mrs. Jones, whose name was Celeste. Of course she had to see everything right away. Never mind that Natalie had been working on her Stevenson book.

Natalie's little books were "dear," a charming outlet for an unmarried young woman—like painting plates. Celeste had never considered the books serious or important. Natalie liked to think that they might give pleasure to children whose lives were otherwise bleak, that she was helping to mold the tastes and emotions of the next generation, that a child might become a better person because he had read her books. Although the books might look frivolous to the casual skimmer, she took them seriously, very seriously. Her mother's attitude made Natalie seethe.

The trousseau was "nice" but why not white? "Remember Veronica's wedding. Was ever a bride more beautiful, a dress more perfect?"

She had wanted to bring Veronica's wedding dress with her in case Natalie wanted to wear it, but Veronica said the dress was too youthful for a bride in her thirties. Perhaps she was right. Celeste folded Natalie's things carefully while she continued to talk about Veronica, her new sofa and the darling children. "I suppose it's too late for you to have children," she said. "Of course we had never planned on grandchildren from you, but still . . ."

Natalie was still seething when she went to bed that night and then she thought about Jack. He, at least, seemed to value her work. Remembering the stormy night when he had read her books, she drifted off into a comforting sleep.

The next morning Natalie told her mother that she had to work to meet a deadline. She went to her studio and locked the doors. Suddenly she was aware of thuds and bangs from her living room and went to discover that her mother was rearranging her furniture.

"Stop it, Mother." She put a table back in its original position. "This is my home. I have arranged the furniture to please me—and Jack, of course."

"I'm not sure I like this Jack," Celeste sniffed. "Under his influence you have become quite rude. You were such a sweet, docile little girl, but once you left home... Your father should never have let you go. Veronica still asks my advice sometimes. Just the other day she asked me if I thought she should have her hair cut short. What are you going to do with your hair for the wedding?"

"Wash it," said Natalie as she strode back into her studio, slamming the door behind her.

The days crept by. With her mother always hovering over her, and the fear that Jack would not show up for the wedding gnawing away inside her, Natalie was in a state of physical and mental disintegration.

SUMMER

FRIDAY MORNING, AFTER A NEARLY SLEEPLESS NIGHT, Natalie staggered downstairs, groping her way toward the coffeepot.

Her mother began humming "Here Comes the Bride." Then she looked at Natalie, put the glasses she wore on a ribbon around her neck up on her nose, and examined her daughter closely. "You look like homemade sin. He's coming today, and you look like that! I can't believe it. Veronica and I are careful to apply a little blusher and mascara before we leave our bedrooms. A woman owes it to those she loves to do her best. Now, let's see what we can do for you."

While Celeste filled the teakettle and searched for tea bags, Natalie poured herself a mug of coffee and toasted a piece of bread, which she could not eat.

Celeste spent the next hour fussing over her ugly duckling. At first Natalie protested. She had to drive to town to pick up the painting she was having framed for Jack. She had decided that the pen-and-pencil set was too impersonal, even for a hired groom, and she had done a second version in oils of the flowering apple trees. It bore the title "Ancient Brides."

Nothing could deter Celeste once she had made up her mind. She stood by while Natalie washed her hair and showered. She put clips, from her own supply, in Natalie's hair and blow-dried the rest of it. She pushed Natalie down on her bed, bunched a pillow under her neck so that her hair would not be mussed and put tea bags on her eyelids. She chattered incessantly, if euphemistically, about a woman's duty to her husband and the joys of marriage.

In the meantime, Natalie lay on the bed in the darkness of the tea bags and fought the nausea of fear. What if Jack did not return? The rest of her family was due that afternoon. Dr. Cedric Forsyth, Veronica's husband, had not been able to leave until after rounds the previous evening, so they were driving through the night, the children sleeping in the back of the station wagon and the doctor, his wife and father-in-law taking turns driving.

When Natalie and Jack left for their honeymoon, Natalie's family would stay on one more night, put the house in order and then drive to the airport, where the old couple would catch a plane back to Ohio. The younger couple and the children would drive on for two weeks on Cape Cod. But what if Jack did not arrive? What if there were no wedding and no honeymoon? *Out, damn thoughts,* Natalie said to herself. Her fears ignored the command and the nausea increased.

"You really should protect your skin when you go outside, Natalie. Skin like yours looks even more sallow when it's tanned, but there's nothing I can do about that now." Celeste sighed deeply. "At least the bags under your eyes will have disappeared. Blusher, eye shadow, lots of mascara. You do have those things, don't you, dear?"

Although Natalie could not see her mother's face, she could read the dismay in her voice. Natalie was a hopeless case. How could she expect Jack to spend six intimate months with her for a mere twenty thousand dollars?

"Now, I'll just run and get the surprise." Celeste's cheerful voice grated on her daughter's nerves.

Within moments she was back, lifting the tea bags from Natalie's eyes. Natalie wanted to snatch them back, to remain a few more minutes in the cool, obliterating darkness. Instead, she sat up and took the silver-wrapped box with the silver ribbon from her mother and opened it carefully. From under layers of tissue paper she pulled out a filmy gown, white, with rows and rows of lace and blue ribbons and ruffles.

"Isn't it lovely? And look, there's more!" Celeste herself reached into the box and pulled out a matching peignoir. "As soon as I saw this set, I knew it was just the thing for you."

Natalie almost laughed. Celeste had always tried to prettify her elder daughter with ribbons and bows. She had outdone herself with this gift, which was definitely not *just the thing*. Natalie had bought herself a silky pink nightshirt with a spray of embroidery on one shoulder. She considered asking her mother to return the lacy garments—they were obviously very expensive. Instead, she kissed her and thanked her with fake enthusiasm. Then she told her firmly that the beauty session was at an end. She was going into town to pick up her painting. Celeste could come along or stay at home, just as she chose.

She didn't have time to choose. They both heard the crunch of tires on gravel. Celeste ran to the window. Natalie held her breath; her family couldn't be here yet, surely.

"I do believe that's the bridegroom," Celeste said coyly. "Wait till your father sees that car. It's the kind he's always admired, totally unsuitable for a lawyer. I do hope you won't be going off on your honeymoon in a car so small. It just doesn't look safe to me . . ."

Natalie joined her mother at the window. As Jack climbed over the door of his little car, Natalie's nausea disappeared.

"Where's my wench?" he shouted to Copper, who ran from the back of the house to greet him.

Natalie flew down the stairs, out the front door and then she stopped, suddenly shy. He winked at her, pulled her into his arms and kissed her firmly. "Come on, babe, the show has begun," he whispered in her ear. Then he slapped her bottom and kissed her again.

They turned to see Celeste watching them with an approving smile. During the introductions, Celeste examined Jack carefully, like a jewel of doubtful authenticity, too good to be true.

Jack began to unload his little car, a carefully restored MG. "I brought my stereo. I know you have an adequate system, but mine is better and I thought we could install it in the bedroom. We'll be spending a lot of time there." He leered at her while Celeste blushed.

He handed her a box and picked up a speaker. "How'm I doing?" he asked when they got to the upstairs hall.

She grinned at him happily. "You're terrific. My mother is captivated already."

"Well, you're not doing so well," he said severely. "Loosen up, will you? We're *supposed* to be madly in love. Don't forget that." He put the speaker in the bedroom and went down for another load.

Natalie just stood there until he returned. "You're right," she whispered. "I do appreciate what you're doing."

He grinned at her and reached into his pocket. "Try this on for size." He handed her a tiny box, which she opened with trembling hands. Inside was a brilliant emerald with a diamond on either side. He took the ring from the box and slipped it on her finger. "My grandmother's. Do you like it? You don't wear much jewelry, but I thought perhaps..."

"It is the most beautiful ring I... But..."

"But nothing. Before my father died he said I was to give his mother's ring to my bride. I'm just following orders." He turned abruptly and went back for another load. Natalie followed.

Jack stayed long enough to drink a mug of coffee while Celeste oohed and aahed over the ring. Then he left to check into his hotel and get ready for the dinner he was hosting. As he was climbing over the door into his car he turned back to ask the ages of Natalie's niece and nephew.

When he was gone, Celeste shook her head, overcome by the wonder of it all. "He's not handsome, but he is obviously smitten with you. And that ring...I'm not sure you recognize its value, Natalie. Unless there's a flaw I can't see, it is worth thousands...or more. You say it was his grandmother's. Tell me about his family."

"Sorry, Mom, I have to pick up my painting. Come on, Copper. We'll leave Mom here to welcome the rest of the family."

"You're giving your new husband one of your own paintings? I'm sure it's very nice, dear, but don't you think you could have given him something a little more valuable? Considering the ring and all..."

"Jack likes my paintings." She held the door for Copper and drove off.

Rick, who was really Cedric Forsyth, Jr., age seven, and his grandfather came out of the woods as Natalie drove up her lane from the highway. Melissa, age five, jumped off the porch with Silver in her arms.

"I'm sorry to have to wait until evening to meet your young man," Natalie's father said, kissing her warmly. "Even allowing for your mother's hyperbole, he must be a paragon." Cedric and Veronica came to the door. "I want to have a little talk with you about your property," her father said. "Let's go for a walk."

They took the children and walked through the woods to the stream. Rick and Melissa waded, Natalie sat on a rock, her father stood. "Rick and I walked around your property, Natalie. I wasn't in favor of your buying this house and land, especially when I had to keep transferring funds to pay for the improvements. I don't know anything about local real estate values, but it now looks to me like you have made a sound investment. What I wanted to ask you today is if you—and your husband—want to take over the management of your inheritance. He may think that I have invested too conservatively."

"No, Dad. If you'll keep on managing it, that will suit us just fine."

He nodded. "If you change your mind . . ."

". . . I'll let you know. I'm glad you like my house. What do you think of my apple orchard?"

"It's in terrible shape. There are a number of dead trees there. I suppose you know that. All the trees need pruning. Are the apples any good?"

"Small and wormy. But the blossoms in the spring are so beautiful that the fruit doesn't much matter." They discussed the property while the children splashed one another and made boats out of bark.

"Dark brown is the river, Golden is the sand . . ." Natalie recited the Stevenson poem for them.

"You're happy . . . You can't know what that means to me," her father said as they walked back to the house.

The divorce would be shattering to this dear man.

Jack was waiting for them on the old-fashioned veranda of the Berkshire Inn when Natalie and her family drove into Lenox. After the introductions, when he must have felt like a manikin in a store window, Jack led them to a table in an alcove off the main dining room. Celeste was in top form, gushing over the flowers that dotted the inn's lawns, the antiques in the lobby and dining room, the table setting.

Jack himself was the perfect host, solicitous of Celeste, deferential to Natalie's father, calling him "sir." When they had ordered drinks, he produced two wrapped packages from under the table which he presented to the children. Each one contained a magic slate and a hand puppet.

Best of all, Jack threw himself into the role of the lovesick Romeo. He kept his arm across the back of Natalie's chair and hugged her to him from time to time. He pecked her cheek. He gazed at her adoringly. He even thanked Celeste for producing such a wonderful daughter.

For just a moment Natalie allowed herself to imagine what it would be like if Jack's adoration were real. The wonder of it was too great. She was content with things as they were. She could not have asked him for a more convincing performance. As she relaxed she threw herself into her role, grinning until she felt like an idiot, squeezing his hand on the top of the table.

Dr. Cedric, accustomed to the role of family prize, was silent while he gulped his first two drinks. Then he ordered a third and began to pry. Why, he asked Jack, had he left his previous job? How did he know he could find another? Was he looking? Jack mumbled and Natalie demanded Jack's attention, asking an inane question about his room at the inn.

Cedric was not to be deterred. "I suppose you like teaching. Why else would you have chosen a job that pays so poorly? Barely more than a garbage collector, I understand."

"I do like to teach," Jack said, turning to Melissa. "Will you call me Uncle Jack? I'm an only child so I never had anyone to call me that."

"Well, you're lucky Natalie has money," Cedric shouted.

Jack was forced to turn back to him to prevent him from blaring information about Natalie's finances all over the dining room.

"Cedric did most of the driving and he's tired," Mr. Jones said quietly. "Forgive him."

Fortunately waiters arrived with their dinners. Mr. Jones took over the conversation during the meal, asking Jack about his car. Rick joined in with questions that demonstrated that he knew more about cars than his grandfather did.

Celeste was curious about Jack's family. She asked about his grandmother and was told that Jack had never met her. That was all.

Veronica was silent. Dressed in white linen with her golden hair swept up into a sleek chignon, she was so lovely that other diners on the way to their tables turned back for a second look. She looks frozen, Natalie thought, Veronica, who had always been so animated. Had the good doctor done that to her? It wasn't until they were having coffee that Veronica turned to her children, hugging each of them and telling them that they could leave the table to walk around outside if they stayed close to the inn. For the first time that day, Natalie glimpsed the old Veronica warmth.

* * *

Jack insisted on driving Natalie home, suggesting that Veronica, who was driving the station wagon, follow so that she wouldn't miss the turnoff from the main highway.

"I'm glad your brother-in-law is not contributing to the gene pool," Jack said as they drove out of town.

"How about Veronica? Don't you hope some of her genes get mixed in?"

"Nice features. But too sleek. Guess that's not inherited." Jack couldn't have said anything more pleasing to Natalie. It was the first time she had ever heard anyone deprecate her sister's looks.

Jack reached into the pocket of his blazer and pulled out a string of beads. "Pearls. The traditional gift, I believe. My grandfather gave them to my grandmother when they were married."

Natalie held them in her hand and stared at the ribbon of highway ahead. "I'll give them back, and the ring," she whispered.

"They are a gift, not a loan." It was too

dark to see his face, but she sensed that he was scowling.

When they got back to the house she took him into her studio and switched on a light over an easel. "This is my wedding gift to you. To remind you of these six months."

He stood looking at the picture from one angle and from another. "God, you're talented," he said at last. "I thought they were arthritic soldiers."

"Ancient brides seemed more appropriate to the occasion," she said.

"Thank you," he said, looking down into her eyes. Then he put his hands on her shoulders.

The children burst into the studio. "Can I go for a ride in your car, Uncle Jack?" Rick asked.

"Me, too," said Melissa. "Uncle Jack," she added.

"I'll drive you to your motel," he said to the children. "See you tomorrow, Natalie," he called back over his shoulder.

* * *

The sun was streaming into the windows, the house was a bustle of activity, and Veronica was standing over Natalie with a mug of coffee when she awoke the next morning.

"Good morning," Veronica said as Natalie scooted up against the headboard. "I left Cedric at the motel and brought the children here so he could sleep. He's been working very hard, you know." Veronica was apologizing for her husband's crude questions the night before. "Mother thought we should have a sisterly chat . . . I don't quite know how to begin . . . We're not in the habit of chatting, are we? I'm sorry about that. We should somehow have managed to be closer . . ."

Natalie patted her sister's hand. "I expect she had a birds-and-bees lecture in mind. Forget it. I read a book. But I appreciate the offer and I'll need lots of advice if I succeed in getting pregnant."

"You're going to try! I'm so glad." Veronica bobbed down and kissed the top of her sister's head. "You know pregnancy and birth are"— she shrugged her shoulders—"wonderful. Of course you pay for the joy during the 'terrible twos' . . ."

"And again during the 'terrible teens,' I understand. Your children were delightful last night, Veronica. You must be a talented mother. You'll be able to teach me a lot. Where are they? I don't hear them."

"I sent them out to gather wildflowers. Mother seems to have the flower situation under control. Doubt that she'll welcome armloads of 'weeds,' but . . ."

"We'll find a place for them. I wanted wildflowers, but you know Mother."

"Has she been just awful? I tried to convince her to stay home until we all came, but I couldn't. Besides, unlike me, you can stand up to her. I envy you, Nat."

"What do you mean?" Natalie was truly astonished. "You're the favorite daughter, the one with the successful husband and the beautiful house and the adorable children. You're the one who gives lovely dinner parties and plays a good game of tennis. You're beautiful . . ."

"And you live your own life." There was bitterness in Veronica's voice. "You have a great talent and it looks to me like you are getting a fine husband. You were very pretty last night and Jack looked like he could eat you up. I think your house is perfect for you. Grandma's furniture looks so right here. Even the ratty old oriental rug."

"Are you happy, Veronica?"

The silence had reached the point where Natalie was about to apologize for asking such a personal question. Finally Veronica said, "I sometimes feel like my life has been molded in plastic—if I could just break the mold now and then—but the children give me joy. Besides, I must like my life. I don't do anything to change it." Veronica went to stand by the window so that Natalie could not see her face. "Get up," she said at last. "This is your wedding day."

Natalie went to Veronica and put her arm around her shoulders. "This isn't the talk Mother had in mind, but I'm glad we've had it. If you ever need me, Veronica, I'm here."

At eleven o'clock Natalie ran through the house and saw that everything was in order.

Veronica had put the children's wildflowers in a huge pitcher and set it on the floor of the entry hall. There were tiny wildflowers in a cup on one of the small tables in the living room. The wedding would take place in front of the window overlooking the orchard. There were huge baskets of florist flowers on either side of the window. The table had been set with Grandma's cutwork linen cloth, and the woman Natalie had hired was busy arranging garnishes and trays in the kitchen for the lunch that would follow the wedding.

The bride, in her silk dress, was pacing the floor of her bedroom when she heard the crunch of tires on gravel and ran to the window to see Jack getting out of his little car. He was wearing a navy-blue suit, beautifully tailored. Who was this man she was about to marry? She had assumed he was poor, but he had astonished her during the last twenty-four hours with a sports car, tailor-made clothes and jewels. Why had he agreed to her charade? Not just agreed—he had thrown himself into the part of the smitten lover. Whatever else he was, he was a gifted actor!

Melissa ran into her bedroom with a tiny rosebud corsage tied to her wrist. "Uncle Jack gave it to me," she said, her eyes sparkling. "And I think it's just beautiful. This is for you." She handed Natalie a white Bible with a sprig of apple blossoms tied on top. Where had he found apple blossoms this time of the year?

Someone started the recording of the Wedding March and Natalie and her niece went down the stairs and entered the living room.

"Dearly beloved, we are gathered together..." The young minister began the familiar service. "... Will you, John, take this woman, Natalie..."

"I do." John's voice was clear and firm.

"And will you, Natalie, take this man, John..."

Natalie opened her mouth but nothing came out. "I... I do," she whispered at last, her heart thudding more loudly than her voice.

"... Whom God hath joined together, let no man put asunder. You may kiss the bride."

When he had kissed her, he hugged her close. "Relax," he whispered into her ear. "It's just for six months."

The photographer snapped pictures, the toasts were made, the luncheon was eaten, the cake was cut. Upstairs she slipped the apple blossoms between the pages of a heavy book, then she pinned on the corsage of tiny orchids which Jack had also given to her. They drove off in a shower of rice.

For better or worse—and for six months—Natalie Jones was Mrs. John V. Berkhardt.

The rocky coast of Maine which Jack had chosen for their honeymoon was the perfect metaphor for the first week of their marriage, filled alternately with crashes and calm.

As soon as he was without an audience, Jack reverted to the taciturn man who had painted Natalie's shed. He responded to her attempts at light conversation with grunts and drove as if his only goal were to get there and get it over with.

The Rocky Point Inn was a converted brown-shingle mansion. Their room was huge with a balcony overlooking a boulder-studded beach. They unpacked their bags in silence except for the steady crash of waves against rocks. A table was set with a cold supper and a bucket with a champagne bottle. He popped the cork.

"Eat and drink and then we'll get down to business." His voice was harsh.

All day Natalie had felt like a stretched rubber band, vibrating with tension. Now when she looked into his frowning face, the rubber band broke. She ran to the bathroom, turned on the tap to obliterate sound, pressed her forehead against the cool tile wall and sobbed.

Suddenly she felt his hands on her shoulders. He turned her around and pulled her close to him. "I'm sorry," he whispered into her hair. "I'm often cruel; I don't mean to be. I just...can't explain. Please come eat your supper. Champagne will help." He held a washcloth under the faucet and wiped the tears and the streaks of mascara from her face.

She began to hiccough. "You're right," she said at last. "This is a business deal. It's just that...You were so wonderful when my folks were around. I just...I don't...I."

"Never mind." He took her hand and led

her to the table and poured the champagne. "To baby planting." He tapped his glass to hers.

"To our baby," she whispered.

They chatted all through supper, about Natalie's family, the wedding, the history of the inn. When they had eaten everything in sight, Jack refilled their glasses with the last of the champagne and rolled the supper table into the hall. Then he went into the bathroom and she could hear the shower running. She stood staring into the black window while he got into bed. Then she took a shower and put on her silky nightshirt and crept into the bed beside him. They drank their champagne sitting side by side against the pillows.

"Now, take off that silly shirt," he said as he turned off the light.

She obeyed. She obeyed his every instruction that night. The man who was her husband reminded her of the musician she had met the night of the storm. He played her softly, gently at first. The crescendo was followed by a quiet coda. She slept. In the middle of the night she awoke and they repeated the symphony with modifications.

He was gone when she awoke in the morning and she ran to the window. She saw him, far below, sitting on a rock and staring out at the sea. She pulled on her jeans and a sweatshirt and ran out to join him. He jumped, startled, as she put her hands on his shoulders. "Thank you," she said, kissing the back of his neck.

He grinned at her and reached out to touch her cheek. Then he pulled back. "Let's have breakfast." The grin was gone.

They spent the day at a craft show, scarcely speaking to one another except when they were admiring the hand-carved wooden toys. While they were eating lobster in a shack overlooking the sea, he pulled five tiny train cars out of his pocket and hooked them together on the table. She pulled four cars out of her purse and they laughed together as they tooted the trains around the table like children.

That night was a repeat of the previous night, but the music was even more beautiful.

On the fourth morning Jack disappeared. His car was gone from the parking lot; his clothes remained in the closet. Natalie spent the day sketching. He returned in time for a late dinner at the inn.

"Where'd you go?" Natalie asked, trying to keep her tone light.

"Had to get away...Maintain perspective."

"I wish I knew more about you," Natalie whispered. "Your parents, your childhood. Your thoughts. What do you really think of me and of what we are doing?"

"I think that you are entirely too nosy."

"You're right," she said after a time. "I'm sorry I pried. I'll try not to do it again."

"My history isn't all that fascinating, anyway. It would be more pleasant for you if I were good at small talk, but you'll have to take me the way I am."

The final days of the honeymoon were passed in near silence—walks on the beach, a movie the day it rained, a drive through the woods. They read mysteries from the inn library. Natalie sketched. As promised, Jack had brought a camera and took pictures of the inn, of her. She took pictures of him. Occasionally they asked a stranger to take pictures of them together.

The silent days were followed by glorious nights.

Copper and Silver were waiting when they returned, the dog with slobbery kisses for both of them, the cat with haughty indifference. While Copper was taking his final run, Natalie moved the hooked rug from beside the bed to her studio. Then she took a sheet from the clothes hamper and put it on the chair. She carried the cat to the chair and led Copper to the rug, patted them both and told them that this is where they would be sleeping from now on.

When she and Jack went up to bed, they latched the door tightly and turned on Jack's stereo to try to drown the sound of the dog scratching at the door and the cat meowing. Morning found Copper on the bare floor beside the bed. Silver was curled up in the bed between them. The door was slightly ajar.

"So which of you clever animals opened the door?" Jack growled.

Silver stood, climbed over Natalie, jumped to the floor and walked sedately out the door, her head held high.

Jack laughed. "That's the snootiest animal I ever met."

Copper, in the meantime, scampered to Jack's side of the bed, jumped up so that his paws were on Jack's chest and licked his face, his tail wagging furiously.

"Good morning to you, too," Jack said. "And to you," he said, turning to Natalie.

"You don't mind having them in here?" Natalie asked.

"Not as much as they mind being kept out. As a matter of fact, I always wanted a dog. I've enjoyed my acquaintance with Copper. He's a companionable sort. Not Silver. She is so self-satisfied that I doubt we'll ever be friends. So be it. I imagine she's the one who opened the door. Don't you?"

Natalie nodded. "You never had a pet?"

"Goldfish. They died."

After breakfast Natalie went back to work on *A Child's Garden of Verses*. Jack disappeared and returned at noon with several different sizes of clippers, a chain saw and a book about pruning. "I'm going to perform surgery on the soldiers," he explained.

When she quit work for the day, Natalie checked his progress on the orchard. He came in and checked her progress on the book. Thus a routine was established. Once a week they phoned Ohio. They went out to dinner occasionally. Natalie planned most of the meals; Jack helped her prepare them. Once they went to the movies.

They had been home for three weeks when Natalie noticed in the paper that a famous Irish flutist would be the guest star at Tanglewood the following Friday night. *What a treat for Jack!* she thought. The next day she invented an excuse to leave the house—she'd run out of carmine, she said—and bought tickets. After dinner she presented them to Jack and then stood back to wait for his response.

It was not the one she had imagined. He just stared at them. "Thank you, Natalie," he said at last, but his shoulders sagged and the corners of his mouth drooped.

Jack always liked to drive his own car, but on the night of the performance he insisted they take hers. They were very nearly late—she'd never known him to take so long shaving—and got to their seats no more than a minute before Osawa raised his baton. And then the music began and Jack relaxed and Natalie enjoyed the concert more for his sake than for her own.

She jumped up at intermission and suggested they stroll across the lawn. Again he hesitated and then followed her. They were just leaving the music shed when she heard someone on the lawn shout, "Hey, Professor!"

Jack's reaction was immediate. He stepped behind her. She turned, but he was off, running back through the shed toward the parking lot. Utterly bewildered, she turned back toward a skinny young man with question marks written all over his face.

"Wasn't that Dr. Berkhardt with you?" he asked Natalie.

Certain that Jack did not want to be recognized by this young man, she simply shook her head and turned away. *How rude!* she thought as she turned back and mumbled an apology.

"Still? After all this time?" the young man said. "If you see him again, please tell him that we wish he'd come back."

"I will," she promised, and then set out to find Jack.

She couldn't. He didn't return to his seat after intermission. Natalie sat through the remainder of the concert, hearing nothing. *Professor. Doctor. After all this time. We wish he'd come back.* What did it mean? Who was this man she had married?

After the concert she walked up and down through the enormous parking lot looking for her car. Would he have taken the car and gone home without her? He wouldn't. She walked for half an hour until the lot was almost empty and her car was visible. Jack was in the driver's seat, his forehead resting against the steering wheel. He didn't say a word to her when she got in, merely lifted his head, started the engine and drove off.

"The young man asked me to tell you that they wish you would come back," she said when they were well away from the crowd and driving along a deserted road. "I don't understand that."

"I don't want you to."

When they got home he climbed out of her car and into his.

"Do you want me to come with you?" she asked.

"No. And don't wait up." He watched her unlock the front door and greet Copper. Then he drove away.

Unable to sleep, she listened to a night talk show until she heard his car, his key in the lock and his footsteps coming upstairs and into the back bedroom.

When she awoke the next morning, Jack was already at work in the apple orchard. She poured some of the coffee he had made—she didn't feel like eating—and took it to her studio, where she was soon lost in her work.

It was after noon when Jack knocked on her door and went in. "I'm not going to explain what happened last night, so don't ask," he said.

"I wouldn't dream of asking. What you do—or did—is hardly a concern of mine." Natalie lied—she was longing for an explanation. *Why was he so damn secretive?*

While she fumed silently he stood in front of her, also silently. "I'm sorry, Natalie," he said at last.

She looked up then into the saddest eyes she had ever seen. Suddenly she knew that Jack was neither criminal nor insane; he had been deeply wounded. By a woman? When he had come on the bicycle, was he escaping the memory of a love lost? He knew so much about how to satisfy a woman in bed...Where was that woman now? Dead, perhaps. Certainly lost to him. What could she say to comfort him? "Would you like to come upstairs?" she asked.

He nodded and she took his hand. It was a first. The first time they had made love in the daytime. The first time she had made love to him.

* * *

The next day it was as if nothing had happened. Natalie worked at her drawing board; Jack pruned the last of the apple trees so that their contorted skeletons were even more pronounced than before. Late in the afternoon she found him in the kitchen with an open cookbook. Jack cooked dinner; Natalie did the dishes. They read for a while and went to bed together.

When they had returned from Maine, he had assumed, without discussion, the mowing and weeding. When he finished pruning the apple trees, he began to do all of the shopping and much of the cooking.

She did not question the changes he made in her diet; actually she did not know that she had been gradually weaned from caffeine until he told her that she had been drinking only decaffeinated coffee for three days.

A week after the concert Natalie woke feeling squeamish. Fortunately Jack was already up and outside. By noon she was feeling physically fine and wondering if she had just imagined the longed-for hint of morning sickness.

She was not really ill; she was too happy to

feel ill. Afternoons she was so tired she began napping in the big chair in her studio. Each new sign filled her with joy. She did not ask herself why she did not share her joy with Jack.

She worked with a new fervor and, although she hesitated to judge her own work, she knew that the illustrations flowing from her brushes were unique. They might just be the best she had ever produced. Jack seemed to share her excitement and took over more and more of the housekeeping tasks.

She was only mildly surprised the first time he served her a big glass of herbal iced tea while he had his usual cocktail before dinner.

"You're pampering me, Jack. I do appreciate..."

"Not you, the baby," he growled.

Did he suspect? For the first time, she considered telling him about the signs of pregnancy. She didn't tell him that night, and by the next night words were no longer required.

She had finished her work for the day and gone out to stroll among the apple trees. She came in through the kitchen door where the aroma of roasting pork assaulted her nostrils and attacked her stomach. She ran through the house and up the stairs, barely making it to the bathroom in time.

Shaking and sweating, she groped her way to the bed with a damp washcloth, which she draped over her face. A few minutes later the cloth was lifted from her face. Jack was scowling down at her.

"I hoped you'd tell me. I kept waiting. Now you don't have to." He pressed another cloth to her face. "I'll be gone in the morning."

She raised herself to her elbows and the room spun and churned. "Don't go yet. Wait till I've seen a doctor." She sank back to the pillow.

"Just as you say. You never gave me my copy of the signed agreement. I assume you did sign it. Where is it?"

She directed him to a drawer in her desk. When she was able to get up and go downstairs, she saw that one copy of the agreement was lying on top of the desk. The other was gone. A light supper was laid out on the kitchen table. Jack was nowhere in sight. He came in late that night and slept in the back bedroom.

The next morning she called Babs to ask for the name of her obstetrician.

"Fast work," Babs said enthusiastically. "Congratulations." She went on to describe the wonderful qualities of her doctor, a middle-aged woman who believed in natural childbirth.

Natalie phoned the doctor's office, hoping there wouldn't be an appointment available for at least three weeks. To her disappointment, the doctor had had a cancellation and would see her the next day.

Jack took her car to be serviced. When he returned, he went upstairs and she could tell from the opening of doors and drawers that he was packing. She went upstairs.

"You could stay around for a while," she suggested. "The agreement was for six months."

"Or until you were pregnant. I've done my stud service. There's nothing more to say. I'll take you to the doctor in the morning. Then it's good-bye, Natalie."

He sounds happy to be going, she thought.

At dinner that night, he handed her a book

entitled *Nine Months*. "Read this. I've underlined the important parts."

She leafed through it and saw that he had,
indeed, underlined it. No caffeine, no alcohol,
plenty of rest, extra calcium.

"Now, about your family. You'll need some
excuse for my disappearance. Tell them I've
gone to the West Coast to look into several
teaching possibilities..."

"Will that be true?"

"That is no concern of yours. Then you can
tell them that I am working out West but will be
home for Christmas..."

"Will you be?"

"I'll probably come by then to check on
you. We can call them while I'm here. Gradually
they'll get used to the idea of my absence.
They'll be so thrilled about the baby that..."

"I'm thrilled about the baby. Are you?"

He shrugged his shoulders. "Glad to know
I'm virile," he said bitterly. "I've been wondering what I should call myself: Surrogate father?
Gigolo? Cohabitator? Not Violator or Rapist, because you not only asked me to service you,
you paid me. Guess Stud is still the best word.

I've performed according to our contract. I'll leave according to contract. You can start the divorce proceedings whenever you like."

She got up from the table and put her arms around his neck while she decided what to say. There must be some words to comfort this bitter man. "I never did like that contract. Why don't we tear it up and . . ."

"You signed it." He took her hands and moved them from his neck to her sides as he got up from the table and turned to glare at her. Moments later he was gone; she heard a whirlwind of gravel as his car sped toward the highway.

Natalie loaded the dishwasher. She scrubbed the countertops, the stove and the sink. She swept the floor. And then she went upstairs and took a bath. She tried not to think and then she tried to think clearly.

Why was Jack so bitter? Why had he agreed to her scheme in the first place? How could any mere "business deal" give so much pleasure? Was it possible that Jack cared for her?

Did she care for him? He was temperamental, that was for sure. Bitter. Sarcastic. Kind.

Tender. Sensitive. She *liked* him. Surely their relationship didn't have to end like this. They could be friends—if they could talk with one another.

She put on her pink bathrobe and went downstairs to wait.

As soon as she heard the crunch of gravel, she went to the door.

"Please come talk with me," she said. "Coffee? Brandy?"

"I've done my work." He pushed past her and ran up the stairs to the back bedroom.

In the doctor's office the next day, he gave one of his great performances in the role of the anxious father. He asked questions about Natalie's health. Would she have any problems? When was the baby due?

"Middle of April," the doctor said.

In the car Natalie suggested a celebration lunch. Jack simply drove straight to her house, where he ran inside and picked up his bags.

"I'm leaving a few things here," he said. "I'll pick them up later."

"How can I get in touch with you?" she asked. "What if something goes wrong? There are more than four months to go on the agreement."

He stared at her. "It doesn't say a thing about impregnating you more than once. I've written a number by the phone. That's in case the doctor needs any information about the sire. It's an answering machine. I'll check with it every now and then. Good-bye, Natalie." He climbed into the car. "By the way, I forgot to congratulate you. Congratulations. I admire anyone who knows what they want and how to get it. You've been remarkably efficient."

"We've been efficient," she corrected. "Thank you, Jack . . . for everything."

He gunned his motor and drove off.

Natalie stood in the doorway watching the MG turn onto the highway. Then she patted her stomach. "Your father has a nasty disposition, but never you mind. He's gone now and we will enjoy the peace we both need." She meant to laugh, but her laugh was a sob.

She went inside and spent the rest of the day working on the scrapbook. There were the two sprigs of apple blossoms, one Jack had given her the day they had their blood tests, the other from her wedding spray. There was the love letter. And there were dozens of pictures from the dinner at the Berkshire Inn, the wedding, the honeymoon and after the honeymoon.

Sometimes she smiled. More often she shook her head, bewildered. Such a strange, secretive man. His spirit seemed to be bent under the weight of some overwhelming sadness, but he was honorable; he had kept his side of the bargain and more. He had charmed her parents and pruned the apple trees and decaffeinated her for the sake of the child, and shown her the wonders of the sexual body. *No, she would not allow herself to think of those nights.* They had not communicated much during the days; she knew no more about him now than she had known when they were married. The silences had not been unpleasant.

"We shared you," she said to the baby within her. "I think he really wanted you; I wonder why when he only expects to see you six hours out of every year."

She heated some soup he had left in the refrigerator, and found that she could not swallow it. She fed it to Copper and Silver and then she made a mug of herbal tea for herself, picked up a mystery she had bought months ago and climbed into bed while it was still light outside.

The words in the book were blurred, but she wasn't crying. Why should she cry? She had everything she wanted: a career, a home and now a baby. She was ecstatically happy.

She lay awake far into the night, listening to the creaks and thumps the house had developed over the summer. She held Silver in her arms; Copper lay on the rug by her side. They were all the companionship she had ever needed.

She slept toward dawn and woke feeling not nauseated, but groggy. In the kitchen she searched the cupboards for *real* coffee. "We need a little pick-me-up," she explained to the baby. She found it at last in an opened can in the freezer and made a pot, which she then threw out. "Sorry, kid," she said. "Your father won't let us enjoy any of the pleasures of life."

She made a mug of instant decaffeinated coffee and drank a big glass of milk.

She sat most of the morning at her drawing board doing nothing. In the afternoon she made a few sketches for the Stevenson book. *Pedestrian*, she said as she tore them to shreds and went upstairs to take a nap.

"We're going to be just fine," she assured the baby.

She didn't even try to work the next morning. Babs came by in the afternoon to see how she'd liked her doctor and to chat about pregnancy and deliveries and babies. "Is your husband pleased?" she asked. "It takes some men a few months to get used to the idea of sharing their wives, so don't be alarmed if he's not. Once the baby grabs his finger..."

"Jack wanted a baby right away. Our ages, you know. Unfortunately he had to go out West. A job..."

Babs was satisfied and promised to check in with Natalie often while he was gone.

That evening Natalie called her parents. They were disbelieving at first and then thrilled. "I can't wait to tell Veronica," Celeste cooed.

"Don't. I want to tell her myself." Natalie discovered that she did want to call Veronica herself. It was not a "duty" call. Something had happened the morning of her wedding; she felt closer to her sister.

Three days later she received a small package which contained a tiny yellow stretch suit and a letter from Veronica:

I wanted to send the first gift. I'm getting together a big box of maternity clothes for you and "first things" for the baby. Don't buy anything until the box arrives. I'm also making a new liner and ruffle for the bassinet. I know it will cost more to ship to you than it would cost to buy new but I want your baby to sleep where my babies slept. Do you understand that? If you want everything new, I'll understand, but I'm hoping...It would mean, somehow, that you and I are as sisters should be—as I want us to be. I know that you meant it when you said that you would always be there for me. I will always be there for you. (You didn't mention Jack when you called but Mother says he is out West job hunting. Is that all right? Am I prying?)

She signed the letter, "Loving Sis and Happy Aunt."

After a few more days sitting in front of her

drawing board producing nothing for the Stevenson book, Natalie put it aside to work on a short novel for ten-year-olds to be illustrated with a few line drawings. She didn't know whether her lack of enthusiasm for the project was due to the quality of the manuscript or the heat. It must have been the heat because she had once read this manuscript and agreed to illustrate it. She must have seen something in it then. The heat was a reality. Day after day in the nineties, and humid. It didn't even cool off much in the evening, which was unusual for the Berkshires.

"This is what they mean about dog days," she told Copper.

Five days into the heat wave, when Jack had been gone for more than a week, the phone rang. "Jack here. How are you?"

"Hi, Jack. I'm fine, thank you. Veronica sent...."

Click. He had hung up.

Natalie was irate. How dare he call like that and then hang up? So he'd said he'd check on her from time to time. So why couldn't they talk? *Damn him. Damn!* He didn't even say where he was. She held the receiver in her hand until it began to buzz to tell her that no one was on the other end. She already knew that. She slammed it into the cradle and began to cry.

"It's not that I want to see him," she told Copper, who was trying to comfort her with wet licks. "I don't. I hired him for a job and he obviously did it well." She began to laugh and then she couldn't stop laughing. She went to the bathroom and dunked her head in a basin of cold water.

Jack phoned again the next weekend and hung up as soon as she said she was fine. She was prepared for his third call. When he asked how she was, she began to tell him in detail. She was taking her vitamins and drinking her milk. She had developed a passion for ice cream and had gained too much weight. The doctor had decided that since Natalie was not yet thirty-five, she would not do the amniocentesis test to determine if there was anything genetically wrong with the baby.

"No, there are certain risks in that, I understand," Jack said without emotion. "So you're getting along okay?"

"Yes, but the car..."

Click.

On the fourth call she didn't answer his question but asked a string of questions herself.

"How are you? And where are you? Are you really looking for a job? Have you found one?"

"I choose not to answer."

"And I choose not to answer your questions, either." Natalie hung up.

She finished the line drawings and mailed them to her editor, who didn't phone when she received them, as she usually did. Instead, she wrote a formal note saying the drawings were acceptable; just acceptable, not terrific.

Again Natalie sat in front of her drawing board and tried to work on the Stevenson book. She painted and threw away everything she produced. She had not produced one usable illustration for what was to have been her major work for the year. Finally she phoned the editor and told her she was pregnant and that the book would be late. It was the first time that Natalie Jones had failed to meet a deadline. Because she was Natalie, the editor did not object.

AUTUMN

IN SEPTEMBER NATALIE RECEIVED AN ENVELOPE WITH a Boston postmark. Inside were copies of pages from Nathaniel Hawthorne's introduction to his *Mosses From an Old Manse*. These were the sentences that were highlighted with a yellow marker:

> An orchard has a relation to mankind, and readily connects itself with matters of the heart. The trees possess a domestic character; they have lost the wild nature of their forest-kindred, and have grown humanized by receiving the care of man, as well as by contributing

to his wants. There is so much individuality of character, too, among apple-trees, that it gives them an additional claim to be the objects of human interest. One is harsh and crabbed in its manifestations; another gives us fruit as mild as charity. One is churlish and illiberal, evidently grudging the few apples that it bears; another exhausts itself in free-hearted benevolence. The variety of grotesque shapes into which apple-trees contort themselves, has its effect on those who get acquainted with them; they stretch out their crooked branches, and take such hold of the imagination that we remember them as humorists and odd fellows.

For the first time, Natalie called the answering machine number and was informed that her message could be as long or as short as she chose. She chose to make it long. She thanked Jack for the paragraphs about the apple trees. She suggested that he might like to come to see the trees in October. Their uniforms would be drab and shabby beside the resplendent oaks and maples but still the old soldiers tried to dress for the occasion.

"According to *your* agreement, I am supposed to present you to the child in a positive light. If you believe in prenatal influences, please tell me how I can present you in a positive light when I have no idea where you are or what you are doing or even why you agreed to my scheme. I only know that I am grateful. The baby will be, too."

Jack didn't phone that weekend or the next.

Natalie had gone to church every Sunday during her childhood and college years. She had become lax when she moved to New York, but she still believed in the teachings of the church and she expected to raise her child in her own faith. She didn't know if she believed in pre-natal influences or not, but she began taking her baby to church in utero.

On his home ground the pale young minister was more dynamic. The hymns brought back happy memories. She was greeted warmly by townspeople to whom she had merely nodded in the past.

One Sunday Babs invited her home for dinner and she met Babs' husband, Bob, and the two older children, both girls, for the first time. They were vegetarians, and Natalie enjoyed the stir-fried vegetables and tofu. But by midafternoon she was sleepy. She apologized to Babs, who sympathized and assured her that the exhaustion period of her pregnancy would be over soon.

As she drove into her lane she saw that Jack's car was sitting in front of her house, empty. Copper did not run to greet her, as was his custom. Catching her breath, she drove into the shed. She was still sitting in the driver's seat trying to put a lid on her excitement when Jack opened the car door.

"Where have you been?" There was anger in his voice and in his face.

"I don't see that you have a right to ask that," she said slowly. "But I'll tell you, anyway. I went to church. Babs invited me to dinner with her family. I got so sleepy—that seems to be a by-product of early pregnancy—that I came home to take a nap." She got out of the car. "I'm glad to see you," she whispered, patting his face.

He turned away from her. "You're right, of course. I had no right to ask. Go take your nap.

I'll mow the lawn. Then we'll phone your folks and tell them the prodigal has returned."

"Have you?"

"No."

"Then let's phone them now and get it over with."

Jack made the call. "Yes, Celeste, I was offered several jobs . . . Yes, I do like northern California, not southern California . . . No, I didn't accept any of the job offers. Actually I decided that I couldn't be away from my bride . . . Yes, indeed, I am thrilled about the baby . . . Boy or girl, either will be fine with me . . . Natalie looks good to me, but the doctor says she's gaining too fast. Here, I'll put her on."

Once again, Natalie marveled at his acting skill. "Have you ever been on the stage?" she asked when she had finished talking with her folks.

He shook his head. "You do look great," he said. "I don't see any sign of the baby."

"According to that book you gave me, it's only the size of a worm." She laughed. "Want a cup of tea? Herbal, of course."

"I'll go mow."

"Don't. I've hired a boy to do that."

"Then I'll be on my way. Good-bye, Natalie. Take care of yourself." He went to the car, got in and drove off without looking back.

She made herself a cup of tea. She had wanted him to come; now she wished he hadn't. She had been too glad to see his hawk-like features, too eager to listen to his voice— she loved his deep voice—too disappointed when he had driven away. The sooner he was out of her life completely, the better.

Color weekend in the Berkshires is the weekend before the fifteenth of October. It arrived in a burst of reds and yellows. On Saturday Natalie and Copper drove up to the southern border of Vermont. The views from every turn in the highway fed her soul.

"Next year," she told Copper, "we'll make this trip with our baby, who will be six months old. You'll like that, won't you? You won't be jealous. You shouldn't be, you know. You'll always be my favorite dog."

Copper, who was riding as usual in the back seat, rested his nose on her shoulder.

They pulled off the road at a rest stop where the view was spectacular in every direction. She gave Copper a dog biscuit and she ate a sandwich and drank a glass of milk from her thermos.

"I had planned to go further," she explained to Copper, "to be gone all day. Frankly I'm tired already. I think we'll head for home. Our baby is wearing me out."

Halfway home, Natalie pulled over to the side of the road to rest for half an hour. She drove on, feeling even more exhausted. Traffic was backed up in Pittsfield so that the drive through the town took almost an hour. She wanted to stop at a supermarket, but she didn't have the energy to get out of the car. The last ten miles seemed like a thousand. Natalie almost ran a red light, stopping with a lurch way out in the intersection. From then on she kept the thumbnail of her left hand pressed into her middle finger, hoping the pressure would keep her alert.

At long, long last she was driving up her

lane. She parked the car as close to the house as possible, switched off the engine, opened the door for Copper and fell forward, resting her head against the steering wheel. She didn't even notice Jack's car parked in front of the shed.

She wasn't aware of anything until she felt Jack's arm around her shoulders. Gently he worked his other arm under her knees and lifted her out of the car. She was too tired to speak or even to smile but not too tired to relish the strength of his arms, the familiar odor of his tweed jacket. He opened the front door without setting her down, carried her straight upstairs and laid her on the bed.

Then he looked down at her with eyes that seemed to share her exhaustion. "So tired."

She nodded, still unable to speak, but overwhelmed with gratitude. So glad . . . so glad that he was there. She put her hand in his.

"Shall I call the doctor?" he asked.

She shook her head and closed her eyes.

When she awoke, the bedroom was dark. She lay for a moment, remembering the ride home, and Jack. He was still there; she could feel his presence. "Jack?"

He switched on the light beside the bed and came and watched her while she sat up, lowering her feet to the floor. The room was swimming, but she had to get to the bathroom. Jack seemed to know. He took her hands and lifted her to her feet, then he pulled her against him and walked her across the room and the hall. He stood outside the bathroom door. When she lowered her head to splash water on her face, black spots appeared before her eyes. Somehow, Jack was there. He patted her face with a towel and led her back to bed. Then he disappeared. Panic. He wouldn't leave her yet, not before she had thanked him.

She heard him call to Copper. Reassured, she lay quietly, listening to his footsteps and the rattle of pans. She was sitting up against the headboard, feeling almost restored, when he appeared with a tray. Two soft-boiled eggs, buttered toast, tea.

He set the tray across her knees and stood watching her eat. When she was finished, he spoke. "Now, tell me where you went and why."

"It was such a beautiful day. I packed a lunch and Copper and I drove up to Vermont to enjoy the colors."

"There are plenty of colors around here. You could have had a picnic in your own yard if you didn't think you could eat without looking at trees." He was angry again.

"But I wasn't tired when I left. And I didn't drive as far as I had intended. I had my lunch and came right back home. I even stopped to rest along the way. But there was a traffic jam in Pittsfield and..." She decided not to tell him about almost running a red light. "Thank you for being here, Jack. I'm sorry you've seen me like this. It's never happened before and I'll certainly be more careful in the future. But for today, I'm glad you were here. I needed you."

"You're an idiot," he growled.

"That's because I never had an opportunity to have a brain transplant." She laughed, feeling suddenly merry.

He frowned and then took her tray downstairs. A few minutes later he was back. "Get ready for bed," he commanded as he lifted the flannel nightie from the hook in her closet.

He sat down on the bed beside her and unbuttoned her shirt. He pulled her turtleneck over her head, and then he stared at her waist. Natalie felt herself blushing. Her jeans were too tight, so that morning she had left them unzipped and had used a huge safety pin to expand the waistband. The gap had been hidden by her turtleneck and shirt.

"My grandmother warned me about occasions like this. She told me never to put myself together with safety pins because I might get hit by a car and have to go to the hospital and what would the nurses think if they saw the safety pins." She laughed but Jack did not. He did not lift his eyes from her abdomen. "That's not one of the seven wonders of the world," she said. "Just the beginnings of a very small baby."

She removed the safety pin, and he got up to tug at the legs of her jeans while she lifted her bottom from the bed. He helped pull the nightie over her head and was smiling straight into her eyes when her head popped through the neck of the gown.

Once again he helped her to the bathroom and led her back to bed. He switched off the light and kissed her forehead. "Thank you, Natalie." His voice was husky.

"Thank *you*." She reached for his hand. "Sit with me for a while?"

"No." He pulled his hand away and closed the door behind him. "I'll be across the hall if you need me," he called from the stairway.

She woke early and got up feeling well and very happy. Before she took her shower, she peeked into the back bedroom, where Jack lay in a tangle of blankets.

"Shhh," she whispered, patting her stomach. "Daddy's sleeping."

She put on the coffee and then drove her car, which Jack had parked in the shed, into town for the papers—the *Boston Globe* for him and the *New York Times* for herself. She picked up cheese and eggs and sweet rolls. She had breakfast under way when he appeared at the kitchen door. He did not respond to her "Good morning" but came and turned her face to the light and stood studying it.

"How are you?" he asked.

"I'm fine. So's the kid. Thanks to you." She kissed his cheek.

He stepped away from her. "So I'll be on my way as soon as we've phoned your folks."

She turned on the burner under the buttered frying pan and waited for it to heat. Then she poured in the eggs, stirring them while she tried to think. She had no right to ask him for any more favors. Still . . .

"You could stay," she said, setting the eggs in front of him.

"We have an agreement." He ate in silence and then got up and went to her studio, where he dialed her parents' number. His performance in the role of doting husband was less convincing than usual, but she doubted that her parents would notice.

When the call was completed he walked directly from the studio to the front door, his car keys in his hand.

"Wait," she called as the door slammed behind him. She ran to the kitchen for the Boston paper and carried it out to his car. "I bought your paper for you," she said, leaning through the window to put it on the seat beside him.

He stared straight ahead for a long time. When he spoke he still did not look at her. "When you decided to have a baby you assumed responsibility for that child's welfare . . ."

"I know that."

"Then act accordingly. No more silly stunts like you pulled yesterday. What if I hadn't been here? You'd still be sitting in that car slumped down on the steering wheel. If you could have seen yourself." Jack was shouting. He turned, glared at her for a moment and drove off.

"Good-bye, Jack," she called after him. "Come again anytime."

Natalie returned to the house to read her *Times*, but the apple trees beckoned her and she went out to the road with her easel and painted the old soldiers in their faded uniforms with a glimpse of her house in the background.

"I should have painted them this summer with their little misshapen apples," she told Copper. "Then I could have done them again in the winter. My version of *The Four Seasons*."

* * *

During the next week the old soldiers began to shed their faded uniforms, and when Jack called on Saturday she told him that his brides were shameless, "standing out there by the road practically naked."

"Cut the chitchat," he ordered. "How are you?"

"I'm fine. I went to the doctor this week and she was even pleased with my weight."

"Good." He hung up.

Natalie worked all of the next week on her Stevenson, and on Friday she destroyed the week's work. Saturday was cloudy and windy and Natalie read a mystery in the afternoon. Her dinner was tasteless. She read a second mystery that night. Several times she picked up the receiver to see if her phone was in working order. It was. She didn't hear from Jack because he didn't call.

Sunday she went to church and was comforted, if only for an hour. She read the *Times* and worked the crossword puzzle. Her mother called in the middle of the afternoon and it took every shred of Natalie's will to try to sound cheerful. The walls of her house were bearing in on her and she put on a heavy jacket, determined to walk off her gloom. What if Jack did call while she was out? He could call again. She walked only to the stream and back, shivering all the way. The heavy clouds were just as oppressive as her walls. That night she went to bed early and begged for obliterating sleep.

Monday morning her gloom and loneliness lifted when she awoke to a world dusted with powdered sugar. As soon as he was out of the door, Copper ran to the road and back. He nosed the snow, trying unsuccessfully to find enough to roll in. Natalie scooped some of it into her hand and threw it at the dog. He caught it in his mouth and a moment later was searching the ground for his ball.

"Silly dog, you've forgotten that snow melts." She threw a rubber ball for him.

Silver scorned the snow and curled up close to the radiator in the studio. Natalie went to work on another, less demanding project, eight black-and-whites for a book for children of elementary school age.

"You're all the company I need," she told her pets while they were having their dinner that night. "You never scowl and you never give orders."

Nevertheless, Natalie longed for human companionship. As soon as the snow had melted the next day, she went to visit Babs, who poured her a mug of herbal tea and then continued kneading bread dough. The older children were in school. The four-year-old was visiting a friend. The baby was taking a nap.

"I haven't seen you for a long time," Babs said in rhythm to her kneading. "Everything okay?"

"Jack's been home." Natalie told her about the drive to see the leaves and her exhaustion.

"Normal." There was silence for a while as Babs slapped the ball of dough. "Smooth as a baby's bottom," she said, placing it in a deep bowl and setting it near the stove. "Has Jack found a job?"

Natalie shook her head.

"I don't want to pry, but is everything all right?"

"Sure." Natalie hoped her voice was light. They spent the rest of her visit drinking tea and talking about Babs' family.

* * *

Early in November there was a real snow that lay on the ground for four days. Housebound, Natalie puttered in her studio, napped and read four mysteries. It was going to be a lonely winter.

"But we'll survive this winter," she told Copper. "And next winter we'll have our baby to keep us company."

Copper rested his head on her foot. Silver jumped into her lap.

"In the meantime, I'll just have to find more absorbing reading material. Maybe I'll read the complete works of Dickens."

And then on the Saturday morning after the storm, Natalie raised the shades in her bedroom and saw Jack's little car parked in front of the shed. She wrapped her robe around her and ran down the stairs and threw open the front door. Jack was sitting on her porch.

"Hi, there. You must be frozen. Why didn't you let yourself in with your key?"

He said nothing, not even "Hello," but followed her into the kitchen. She suggested that he sit at the table, but he stood in the middle of the kitchen so that she had to dodge around him on every trip between the sink and the cupboards. When the coffee maker was going, she asked him if he wanted eggs. He didn't answer. "Toast, then," she said, and put slices of bread in the toaster and poured glasses of orange juice. Still, Jack did not speak. Finally Natalie went and stood directly in front of him.

"Good morning, Jack," she said sweetly.

"I'm moving back. I don't care what you say, you shouldn't be here alone this winter. We've already had one storm and we're going to have more. This is going to be one of the worst winters on record."

"How do you know?"

"The squirrels have unusually bushy tails."

Natalie laughed. "And you believe that is an omen, of course."

"It also has something to do with cycles. Blizzards are due this winter, so there is no point in arguing with me. I have a job to do that requires a computer. I've ordered it sent here, and I will set it up in the back bedroom. I will stay here in this house until the baby is born. I know it's not in our agreement. I'll add a codicil to that. You can't stop me." He was shouting at her.

"Do you hear me arguing? I'll be glad to have company this winter." She reached up and kissed his cheek.

He pushed her away. "None of that. I intend to keep to the back bedroom. There need be nothing personal between us . . ."

"You don't think a baby is personal?" Natalie giggled.

Jack scowled. "It will be a simple business arrangement. I need a place to work and you need a keeper and a nurse."

"I do not need a keeper and a nurse. I am neither mentally nor physically ill. I'm pregnant and I *need* a friend."

"Okay. I'll be your friend," he growled.

She poured the coffee, buttered the toast and sat down. He lowered himself into the chair opposite her.

"Look, Jack, if you're going to be here all winter, I'd appreciate it if you'd send your bear self into hibernation. The baby and I need peace. That's what your blessed book says." Her eyes felt moist, which was absurd; she was glad, not sad.

He stared at her as if she'd said something earth-shattering. "You're right, of course. I'll try very hard not to upset you. You really don't mind my moving back?"

She shook her head. "I'm glad," she said at last. "To tell you the truth, I've been lonely. I got used to having you around."

"I'll take you out to dinner tonight." He extended his hand across the table. "Friends?"

"Dear friends."

Natalie wore a maternity dress for the first time that night, one of Veronica's, white wool with a high neck and long sleeves. For color she added a bright paisley scarf and went downstairs feeling self-conscious.

"Nice," Jack said. "Very nice." He got the camera and took her picture for the scrapbook.

While they ate at a Polynesian restaurant on the Lenox road, Jack asked about her work and expressed sympathy when she told him that she had made no progress on the *Child's Garden of Verses*. She asked him if he had really been to California. He had, two weeks in the Frisco area, where he had lined up the statistical job he was working on.

"Where else have you been?" she asked.

"That's really none of your business, Natalie."

"So much for that topic of conversation," she said sarcastically. "Can you tell me about your computer? Or is that a secret, too?"

Ignoring her tone, he launched into a discussion of his computer, using a vocabulary that was like a foreign language to Natalie. That she couldn't understand what he was talking about didn't matter. He was talking and they were comfortable together.

When they returned home, he sent her upstairs while he waited for Copper to come back from his run. She put on her pink nightshirt, sprayed herself with cologne and climbed into bed to wait.

At last she heard him call to Copper and the two came upstairs together. Copper came directly to his rug beside the bed. She heard Jack go into the back bedroom, where the bed was stripped to the mattress. She heard him rummaging through the linen closet. Natalie sighed, disappointed, when she heard him shut *and lock* his door.

The computer arrived the next week and once again their days fell into a routine. They seldom had breakfast or lunch together. They worked in their own rooms. They took turns preparing dinner and ate together. In the evenings they watched television or listened to records or read. Sometimes he asked about her work and she showed him finished illustrations. Once again the Stevenson book was going well. He sometimes talked about his computer but never about the work he was doing. They slept apart.

He asked her, reluctantly she thought, if she wanted to go to the Berkshire Inn for Thanksgiving dinner and responded eagerly when she suggested that they prepare their own feast. He'd make a pumpkin pie. No, he'd never baked a pie but he could read, couldn't he? He could follow instructions.

They went shopping on Wednesday and Jack selected a twenty-pound fresh turkey. Natalie lifted it from the cart, put it back in the case and selected a five-pound roasting chicken.

He picked up his turkey and returned it to the cart.

"We'd be eating turkey all winter. Surely a chicken is more appropriate for two."

"Three," he said, putting the chicken back in the case. "I like left-over turkey. We can freeze some of it and give the rest to Copper."

"That's so impractical," Natalie protested.

"So it's impractical. I want a Thanksgiving-sized bird."

She shrugged her shoulders. "Then you'll have to give in to me and eat turnips. Thanksgiving isn't Thanksgiving without turnips."

He grinned his agreement.

They spent all of Thanksgiving morning working side by side in the kitchen. Jack tackled his pie as he had tackled the shed, with awkward concentration and determination.

Happily she set the table in the living room with her grandmother's damask cloth and napkins. She arranged a centerpiece of bronze chrysanthemums and got out her best china. The turkey, browned to perfection, looked silly on a table set for two. Jack had to laugh when he saw it, but he took a picture of the table before they sat down to eat.

"We should say grace," she announced.

"I can't do it."

"I can," she said, bowing her head and reaching across the table for his hand. "Dear God, Jack and I are grateful for all of our blessings, for food and shelter, for work, but most of all we are grateful for our baby. May it be born healthy, and help us to help it to grow strong and happy. Thank you. Amen."

Jack squeezed her hand.

Natalie commented that the turkey was better than any chicken could have been. Jack said her cranberry sauce was the best he had ever eaten. He even liked the turnips, which he thought he hated. And then he brought on his masterpiece, cut a wedge and handed it to her, watching as she took the first bite.

She held it in her mouth for a moment before she swallowed and smiled into his anxious eyes. "My grandmother was famous throughout Ohio for her pumpkin pie," Natalie said, "but it couldn't compare to this. I pronounce you master pumpkin pie chef."

Jack beamed like a happy child.

When they were stuffed, they cleared the table quickly and went for a long walk. As they walked, Natalie slipped her hand into his. He held it.

"When I was a child we always had a gathering of the clan for Thanksgiving, all of the aunts and uncles and cousins and some people we called aunt and uncle but who weren't related at all. Where did you eat Thanksgiving dinner?"

"At the Parker House. With my mother and father."

"Thanksgiving dinner at a hotel?" She was incredulous.

"I had a few Thanksgiving dinners in school dining rooms and twice I went home with classmates. They were big affairs like you describe, but I felt like an outsider. This was the best Thanksgiving in my life. Thank you, Natalie."

Natalie was speechless, but when they returned to the snug little house she regained her voice to make a suggestion. "If you would play your flute, it would be the ending to a lovely day," she said.

While he played, she lay contentedly on the couch. At last he stopped and made a suggestion of his own. "Why don't you read to me? If you feel up to it?"

"What would you like to hear?"

"Your choice. I didn't ask you what you wanted me to play."

She went to her studio, returned with a book, switched on the light by the sofa and began to read: *"Alice was beginning to get very tired of sitting by her sister on the bank and of having nothing to do: once or twice she had peeped into the book her sister was reading, but it had no pictures or conversations in it, 'and what is the use of a book,' thought Alice, 'without pictures or conversations?'"*

When she had read Lewis Carroll's words for a long time and her voice was becoming husky,

Jack came and sat beside her, took the book and continued the story. She leaned against his shoulder listening to the familiar words and then, suddenly, she felt a flutter, like butterfly wings. She stayed perfectly still until she felt it again. And again.

"What is it?" Jack whispered, laying aside the book.

She took his hand and placed it on her abdomen. "Can you feel it?"

He pulled his hand away and then put it back. "My God. Oh my God!" He sounded as if he were praying.

For a long time they remained silent with Jack's hand on her. At last Natalie sat up. "I guess the baby has gone back to sleep," she said, looking up at Jack.

Behind his black glasses there was awe. He didn't speak for a long time. Then he blinked and shook his head.

"Do you like the name Alice?" he asked. "It's old-fashioned but..."

"Alice? Yes, Alice!" She rapped gently on her stomach. "Are you there, Alice?"

"You get an answer?"

"No." She sighed.

"Maybe it's not an Alice. Maybe it's a boy child. We'd better find a nonsexist name until we know what's in there. Like Leslie or Francis."

"How about Dodo?" she suggested, since they had just read about Dodo.

"Dodo it is." He laughed and stood up, taking her hands to raise her. He stood smiling down at her.

"Sleep with me tonight," she whispered. "Please."

He turned away.

"We're lawfully wedded, you know." She put her hand on the back of his neck.

"Until April." He turned and then he grinned and picked her up in his arms. He carried her up the stairs and laid her on her bed and kissed her gently and then not so gently.

Natalie was haunted by the picture of a little boy in horn-rimmed glasses eating Thanksgiving dinner with two stern adults at the Parker House hotel. Had his childhood Christmases been more cheerful? Probably not. She vowed to give their Christmas together a story-book quality.

He cooperated wholeheartedly, agreeing without hesitation to go with her to shop for her family. He gravely considered the right truck for her nephew, the right building set for her niece, the book on classic cars for her father, the lacy blouse for her mother.

When they had selected the blouse, Jack led her to a display of shawls. "The color isn't as important as the feel," he said.

Bewildered, Natalie began fingering shawls. Jack never looked at the price tags but bought the softest one, which was cashmere, in a lovely shade of blue. The price was astronomical!

As they were driving home, Natalie asked who the shawl was for.

"My mother."

"Your mother? Your mother is living?" She could hear anger rising in her voice. "You said you had no immediate family. I guess you didn't want her to know about me and our sham wedding. It's too bad you couldn't have thought about how *she* might feel to be denied knowledge of her only grandchild. Or does she have others? You said you were an only child. Are you? It's obvious that I know nothing about you, but I always thought—stupid me—that you were honest."

He drove into the shed before he spoke. "My mother could not have come to our wedding. She doesn't *know* anything or anyone anymore. And she never did like children much. She was an accountant who didn't count on me. I was born just before her forty-first birthday. I've often wondered why she didn't have an abortion. Probably my father wouldn't let her." Jack's voice was incredibly bitter.

"Where is she now?"

"In a nursing home outside of Boston. A fine institution of its type. She doesn't know me when I visit, but she's still adding numbers. The only thing I can do for her is provide her with columns of numbers—the computer is good for that—and pay other people to care for her."

"Oh, Jack." Natalie was overcome with shame. "I'm sorry for what I just said. Really sorry. I . . ."

"Forget it." He climbed out of the car, his arms filled with packages.

"The shawl is a thoughtful gift. I suppose, like most old people, she's usually cold. She'll love the feel of it," she babbled as she followed him to the door with the rest of the packages.

They ate dinner in silence while Natalie cursed herself for her tactlessness. When they had cleared the table, she asked if he wanted to talk about his father.

"He's been dead for ten years. He was older than my mother. He wanted to be a concert violinist but he was an engineer. Nice old man. He began taking me to the Boston Symphony concerts when I was five. Every Saturday afternoon. People always thought he was my grandfather. He'd have liked to know about you and the baby." Jack smiled at her, but his eyes were filled with deep sadness.

Natalie reached across the table to pat his hand. He grabbed hers and held it. "I know you'll love Dodo, Natalie. Just make sure that Dodo knows that you love him. Promise me that."

She nodded sadly, thinking of her own parents. She had been critical of them when she should have been grateful for their love. They hadn't always understood her, but they had tried to make her happy. Christmases had been joyous.

"Promise aloud," he commanded.

"I promise that I will love Dodo and will demonstrate my love daily, so help me God."

"So help you God," he repeated after her. "So when do we wrap the Ohio presents?"

Jack loaded the dishwasher while Natalie laid a supply of trimmings and paper on the living room floor. She wrapped the box with the truck in red paper and drew wheels with a felt-tipped pen. She put doors in the back and Rick's name along the side in big block letters.

"Just like the trailer of a moving van," Jack said, holding it in his hand and examining it from all sides.

She handed him a pen and he carefully wrote, "Merry Christmas from Aunt Natalie and Uncle Jack," below the child's name. Then he examined it again.

She wrapped the other presents and went upstairs for a pottery mug she had bought earlier in the year for the good doctor. "He won't think much of it, but it's the best I can do. I used to give him fancy brandy for Christmas. Now I don't think that's such a good idea."

"What about your sister?"

"I don't know if she'll like my present, either. She may think I'm interfering." She picked up a college catalogue, slipped a piece of paper inside and rolled it and wrapped it to look like a firecracker. "I'm giving her the college course of her choice. Now for the shawl. What's your mother's favorite color?"

"I don't know. Probably black. Accountants love black ink. But we don't have to wrap it. A nurse will open it for her."

Ignoring him, Natalie picked up the box with the shawl. "You say she likes numbers. Do you have any used computer paper, with numbers on it?"

He went upstairs and returned with a stack of paper. She selected the sheets that were completely covered with numbers and used them to wrap the box with the shawl. She put a huge green bow on top and was slipping it into a mailing bag when Jack stopped her.

"Not yet," he whispered. "Tomorrow. Just before we go to the post office. Tonight I'd like to look at it." He took the box in his hands and turned it over and over. Then he set it on the table and came and sat on the floor beside Natalie. He held her in his arms stroking her hair and she knew that she was comforting him in the same way that Silver had often comforted her.

The week before Christmas she suggested that they look for a suitable tree in the woods.

"We always bought our trees at the local lot, but cutting a tree from our own land seems to me to be so wonderfully New England. Our pines are probably as misshapen as the apple trees, but still . . ."

They tramped through the woods and discovered that Natalie was right. These trees, grown in the wild, were not perfect specimens by a long shot. But they found one which seemed to be the right height, and full on two sides. They could put it in a corner. Jack chopped it down and hauled it home. What had seemed small beside its brothers was enormous in their living room. It touched the ceiling and dwarfed the furniture. Jack's eyes glowed as he stood back to survey it.

That afternoon Jack did the shopping and came home with strings of lights shaped like little candles and cranberries and popcorn.

"I never did this before," Jack said as he arranged and rearranged the lights until they were as symmetrical as the tree would allow. He hung the small ornaments from the tree Natalie had once had in her apartment, and the larger ornaments that he had bought.

They strung popcorn and cranberries on three successive evenings.

"I never did this before, either," Natalie said. "Somehow, I was under the impression that it was an easier job. I never considered that it might be difficult to pierce cranberries and that popcorn breaks."

At last they could pronounce the tree decorated. Jack went upstairs and came back with a huge box. He hung his head like a naughty child.

"You'll think this is silly, but . . . Once when

I was a child I visited a classmate who had a huge tree with an electric train running in circles under it...I thought it was...I've always wanted...Besides, you can put it away after Christmas for Dodo..."

Natalie threw her arms around the embarrassed man. "For years I asked for a train for Christmas, but my parents just laughed. Trains aren't for girls, they said. I had a cousin who had the most wonderful set in the whole world, but he wouldn't let me handle the controls. Will you let me run your set?"

"Our set." He kissed the top of her head, then cut the string and opened the box and began to assemble the track to encircle the tree. They sat on the floor and played with their train like a couple of seven-year-olds.

"Dodo is leaping for joy," Natalie announced.

The next day, Natalie insisted on shopping alone. She arrived home to find Jack up to his elbows in flour. He was baking cookies.

"We have a very important decision to

make," Natalie announced. "Shall we open our presents on Christmas Eve or Christmas morning? When I was a child, Santa Claus came while we were at church on Christmas Eve. We had more presents when we got to Grandmother's on Christmas Day. When did you have your presents?"

"Christmas Day, whenever we got around to it but before we went to the Parker House for dinner."

"Did you always go to the Parker House on special occasions?"

"My mother didn't like to cook," Jack said flatly.

"So what shall we do? I don't suppose you'd like to go to the candlelight service at . . ."

"I'm an atheist by birth, but, yes, I'd like to go to church with you and Dodo. Maybe Santa will arrive while we're gone."

And so it was a special Christmas. While Jack got out the car, Natalie fetched her stack of presents from the back of her closet and laid them under the tree with the presents that had already arrived from her family and a few of her New York friends.

The church was decorated with banks of poinsettias and white candles. The service was simple: the reading of the Christmas story, the singing of the old carols. It was beginning to snow as they left the church.

At home, Jack made her wait in the hall with her eyes closed while he went to check on Santa. She heard him rushing around, from the living room to the kitchen and back. Then he put Christmas carols on the stereo and started the train in motion.

"He's been here," Jack announced, and she turned to see him opening a split of champagne, which popped joyfully. "You and Dodo may have one glass, I'll drink the rest," he said.

A huge teddy bear sat under the tree with a card between its paws. "Merry Christmas to Dodo from Daddy and Mommy." Beside the bear was a catnip mouse for Silver and a rawhide bone for Copper. There was also a large, beautifully wrapped box, which Jack handed to her.

He stood back and watched as she carefully removed the ribbon and paper, lifted the lid off the box and separated the layers of tissue paper. Holding her breath, she drew out a burgundy-red velvet robe, lined with white silk. It had a high mandarin collar and would hang loosely from the shoulders. She felt choked as she fondled the folds.

"Put it on."

"I wish I were pretty enough to do it justice," she said more to herself than to him. She stepped out of the white wool maternity dress and into the luxurious robe. "It's beautiful, Jack. And a perfect fit. There's even room for Dodo to grow."

"I think you're beautiful," he said.

She knew she would cherish those words for the rest of her life.

Jack was surprised that there were presents for him from her family, and he obviously took special pleasure in the pencil container that Melissa had made from a tin can. Natalie gave him a book that contained a cardboard village to be cut out and assembled for the train set, a semaphore, a biography of Nathaniel Hawthorne, a box of dried fruit, and the framed painting entitled "Aging Brides in Fall Drab."

* * *

Christmas morning there were two more presents under the tree—a rattle for Dodo and a carved music box that played Brahms' lullaby for Natalie.

They spent most of the morning cutting and assembling the village and arranging it around the train track. When they had eaten their roast beef dinner with another of Jack's pumpkin pies, they went for a walk in the snow.

"This is the kind of Christmas I always dreamed of," Jack said. "Thank you, Natalie."

More words to cherish!

WINTER

FOR THE FIRST TIME IN HER LIFE, NATALIE HAD FUN on New Year's Eve. She and Jack went out to dinner at a small Italian restaurant and then to a movie. At home Natalie put on a record of oldies and they danced. Neither of them was a good dancer; it didn't matter. They toasted the new year and their baby with herbal tea. And then they went to bed.

The following week when the phone rang, the call was for Jack, the first he had received at her house. His hands shook as he reached for the phone. He said hello, listened for a few minutes, then said he'd be there that night.

"Mother's nursing home," he explained. "They're the only people I gave this number to. She has pneumonia and they've transferred her to the hospital. They don't expect her to live. I've got to go, Natalie. I hate to leave you in January."

"I could come with you."

"I don't want you." He spoke emphatically.

Twenty minutes later he was gone. He called the next night to say that his mother had died. He had to see her lawyer. He'd be home in a few days.

"What about the funeral?"

"She didn't want one; neither did my father. She'll be cremated and the ashes put in a crypt beside his."

"You're not even going to have a prayer said for her?" Natalie was shocked.

"She was an atheist, remember?" He hesitated. "Maybe you . . . Could you . . . ?"

"Yes, Jack. I could say a prayer for your mother. Is there anything else I can do?"

"No. How's Dodo?"

"Active."

"Good."

While he was gone, Natalie tried to work on her Stevenson. Work went badly. Why, she paused to wonder, could she only do good work on it when Jack was in the house? There was no answer to that question.

She decided to tackle her income taxes instead, and laid out all of the receipts and check stubs and tried to organize them. Until she had bought the house, her father had taken care of her taxes. With the house, she had decided to declare her emancipation. Adults could surely do their own taxes. The first year she'd ended up dumping everything into the lap of an accountant on April 12. This year she would do it herself if it killed her.

It might very well kill her, she decided two days later. Totally confused, she laid her head on top of her pile of papers and wept in frustration. She was so overwhelmed by the mess on her desk that she didn't hear Jack's car in the lane.

He stood for a moment in the studio doorway, then rushed to her side and took her in his arms. "What's the matter? Are you ill? Hurt?"

"The United States government is killing me," she wailed, and then she laughed.

Jack looked down at the papers on her desk and the form that had so many X's and arrows and lines in the margin that even she couldn't make sense of it anymore.

"I don't believe it. You're a grown woman and you can't do your own income tax. Look at those numbers scattered all over the sheet. What are these columns of figures that aren't even straight?"

"Business expenses."

"What's the question mark doing there?"

"I bought a baby gift for a girl who works for one of my publishers and I can't remember what I paid for it."

"Look at your check stubs."

"I paid cash."

"You ninny. You absolute ninny! The IRS requires simple records and arithmetic, nothing more complicated than an intelligent twelve-year-old should be able to do."

Natalie tapped his shoulder until he looked

at her. Then she smiled sweetly. "Hi, Jack. I'm glad you're home."

He gasped. "Good God!" His hands were shaking. "I've done it again." He turned and strode out to his car. Moments later she heard the storm of scattered gravel.

"I hope your daddy slows down before he gets to the highway," she said to her baby. Then she picked up a pencil and drew an angry bear with black glasses. His fangs were bared and he was shaking his paw at a little pregnant rabbit who sat huddled beside her hole. She propped the drawing against one of the steps at eye level and took a book and went to bed. At last she turned off the light and went to sleep.

When she awoke there was a note propped up against her alarm clock:

Dear Natalie, I belittled you and I am truly sorry. I don't know why I do that. Perhaps it would be better if I left now, to give you and the child the peace you require.

She scrawled across the bottom of his note: "All is forgiven. Don't go." She put the note on the pillow in the back bedroom, where he slept.

"I'll do your income tax for you," he said when he came downstairs "as an act of penance." That's all that was ever said about the incident.

She knew that he was biting his tongue when he asked for records that she didn't have or for explanations of incomplete notes in her files. She was a lousy record keeper. She didn't need him to tell her that. At last the odious job was done. Jack had found deductions she'd never heard of; she had to pay less on a greater income than she had paid the year before.

When the forms and check were in the mail, he presented her with an accordion file, each compartment carefully labeled. Then he opened the bottom drawer of her desk and pulled out the top piece of paper.

"What have we here?" he asked. "A bill for pens and paper. What do we do with it? We drop it in the compartment labeled 'Business Supplies.' Simple, isn't it?"

It did look simple. He deposited each of the few receipts she had accumulated since the first of the year in the proper compartment.

"That's all there is to it. Just put the receipts

where they belong and next year at tax time you'll be able to prepare your own taxes just like that." He snapped his fingers. "Will you use it?"

She agreed, although she doubted that her tax forms would ever be a snap.

She wished she could have seen his returns; then she might know what he really did for a living. She was convinced by this time that he had never taught high school math. But he worked on his taxes in his room, which she was never invited to enter. She'd actually heard him turn the lock when he went in. It irritated her to the point of irrationality. One day she told him so.

"I don't know what you keep in that room, but you don't have to lock it in. I'm really not all that curious about what you do in there. You've got a secret. What makes you think I care about your petty little secrets? But if you want to be sure I stay out, all you have to do is say 'Stay out.' But no, you all but spread explosives in the doorway. It makes me so . . ."

"So mad?" he asked eagerly. "Congratulations, Natalie. I was beginning to think that nothing could make you mad. I'm glad to know that you have the capacity for anger." He paused. "I'm also glad you don't let it out often. One temperamental person in the house is enough."

A few days later he invited her to his room at four o'clock for a "business discussion."

Totally mystified, Natalie knocked on his door at the appointed time. He greeted her formally and led her to a chair opposite his bare desk, seated her and then himself.

"Now, Natalie," he said slowly, "you may very well think that I am entirely too presumptuous, but I am concerned that you may not have fully considered the costs of raising and educating a child. I now know something about your income."

"Everything was right there for you and the government to read."

Ignoring her interruption, he went on with what sounded like a prepared speech. "You have a very good income from your books . . ."

"Some years it's good and some years it isn't."

"There was interest, so you must have investments."

"My grandmother left me a legacy."

"Do you know what a child costs? Shoes. I saw the smallest shoes I have ever seen anywhere and they were twenty-six dollars. Twenty-six dollars!"

"Babies that small don't need shoes."

"Do you think bigger shoes are cheaper than little shoes?"

"Truth to tell, I hadn't thought much about the cost of shoes."

"I was afraid of that. What about Dodo's college? Have you thought about that?"

"Of course not. Dodo hasn't been born yet. Eighteen years from now, I'll think about it. Okay?"

"Now is when we should be thinking about it, and saving for it. What if Dodo wants to dance, or study music?"

"I'll have to provide lessons. But maybe Dodo will have no talent."

"And maybe Dodo will be as talented as you are."

"So I'll buy a set of sixty-four crayons. You can bring her stacks of used computer paper. She can draw on the backs of it."

Jack sighed. "I do wish you'd be serious, Natalie. I'm trying to help you provide for the child's future. I'd like to help . . ."

"No. This was my idea. I'll take care of educating Dodo. Don't worry. Suppose I open an account right away and add whatever you say each year, one thousand dollars, more?"

"Ask your father to help you invest it. He may suggest zero coupon bonds. Now, there is one other thing. Have you a will, Natalie?"

"A will? Why would I want a will? I'm pregnant, not mortally ill."

"Prudent people have wills. You must promise me to have one drawn as soon as Dodo is born . . ."

"Okay." Natalie agreed hastily and rose to her feet, anxious to end the discussion.

"Sit down," Jack commanded. "I want to ask you to consider granting me a special favor. Don't make a decision now but think about it.

I'd like to have you name me as guardian in case anything happens to you."

"Of course. If that's what you want. We don't have to discuss that . . ."

"I wouldn't want your doctor brother-in-law to raise my child, and your parents are too old and I . . ."

"Oh, Jack, you worrier. You're acting just like a . . . just like a . . ."

"Father."

"Yes. A very dear, concerned, loving father." She stood then and kissed him on the top of his head. "And thanks for inviting me to your office, not that there's anything to see."

Natalie woke in the wee hours of the night. When she came back to bed, the bedside light was on and Jack was facing her, his head propped up on his hand.

"Did I wake you, Jack? I'm sorry." She turned off the light.

"I was awake. I haven't slept. Maybe I am a worrier, but there's something else."

"Fire away."

"It's about... talent. Some people, some groups of people, lose their ability to do... what they were good at... when they get older."

"Who?" She lay thinking for a moment. "Doctors? Surgeons? A surgeon couldn't operate if he had palsy. Who else? Not musicians. Rubenstein was playing at ninety. Who?"

"Mathematicians. Almost all mathematicians have made whatever contributions they have to make while they are very young—except John von Neumann..."

"Who?" Natalie laughed and put her head on Jack's shoulder. "Who? Who? Who? I sound like an owl."

Jack chuckled. "Von Neumann worked on early computers. But that's beside my point. What I want to know specifically is do artists lose their talent?"

"Picasso? Monet?"

"Hadn't thought of them."

"Did you really mean illustrators? Are you asking me if I expect to be on welfare before Dodo is raised?"

"Something like that."

"It's three o'clock in the morning, Jack. Everyone worries about silly things at three o'clock in the morning. But, to respond to your worries so you can get some sleep, Marguerite de Angeli, whom I especially admired, had a book published when she was in her eighties. I expect to be able to do my thing for many years."

She thought about the months during the autumn when she could do nothing on her Stevenson verses. "Sometimes I feel like I'll never do anything worthwhile again. I felt that way this fall—and again while you were in Boston. But the feeling passes. On the whole I'd say that my work is getting better as I mellow into old age. Dodo is tapping out a message of agreement. So believe me, Jack, this child is not going to be begging on a street corner. I promise."

Natalie had signed up for a childbirth course which would begin early in February, but when February arrived so did the bitter weather that Jack had predicted. He would not let her go to the grocery store, let alone drive all the way to Pittsfield at night for her class.

"Maybe you could drive me," she suggested. "You wouldn't have to go in. Just drop me at the door."

"No. The roads are treacherous. Get your priorities straight. Your safety is the important thing. Yours and Dodo's. I'm not going to risk an accident just so you can attend a class."

"But, Jack..." How could she make him understand how important this was to her? "I want a baby more than anything in the world, Jack. You know that. But I also want to experience *having* a baby. I...It's part of being a woman...It's..." She shook her head. She couldn't put her feelings into words.

He patted her shoulder. "If the roads clear, I'll take you."

"But I'll have missed the first session." Natalie felt tears rising.

"So be it. Besides, I thought the father had to participate in natural childbirth."

"Would you want to be there?" The threat of tears vanished. "Would you?"

"I don't know. Blood...pain...I don't know if I could deal..."

"That's not part of the bargain, Jack. I didn't *expect* you to be here this winter at all. It will be wonderful if you will just drop me off at the hospital. You can wait here at home and I'll phone you when it's all over."

Jack wouldn't even let Natalie drive the few miles to church. The first Sunday in February he drove her himself and then picked her up after the service. The second Sunday, Jack got out of bed, raised the shades, shivered and ran back to bed, pulling Natalie to him for warmth.

"Might just as well stay right here." He laughed. "We can't even get our papers."

"Why not?" She yawned, lying contentedly in his arms.

"Because there's at least a foot of snow in the lane. I told you that this was going to be a terrible winter. I was right. It's still snowing."

"I don't think this has been such a terrible winter."

"I don't, either." He kissed her cheek. Then he shook himself and pushed himself away from her and out of bed. "I'll get the breakfast, then I'm going to spend the day with my computer."

Natalie sighed. Why couldn't he just relax and forget that their marriage was a temporary one? Why could they cuddle only in the dark? Because he didn't want to become involved, obviously. How much more involved could two people be?

She asked herself another question: What should she do about Valentine's Day? Thanksgiving, Christmas and New Year's Eve had been highlights of her life—and Jack's too; of that she was certain. But Valentine's Day was different. It was the holiday for lovers. They were not lovers—except in a physical sense. But still . . . Should she just ignore the day? Would he remember it?

"I'm putting the eggs on," he called from the bottom of the stairs.

Natalie got up and stepped into her velvet robe. The silk lining caressed her skin. "We look quite lovely in this robe," she said, patting her baby.

Jack spent the day in his room upstairs.

Natalie spent the day in her studio with red paper and all the scraps from her collage box.

Three days later, Valentine's Day, it stopped snowing, but the little red house was window-sill-deep in drifts. Jack had kept a small area outside of the back door cleared so that Copper could get out, but even the big dog seemed content to spend most of his time inside.

After breakfast, Jack took a pound of hamburger out of the freezer. "That's it," he said. "Tomorrow, tuna fish."

"I'll make a meat loaf," Natalie announced. "Good for two days. We still have two potatoes. I'll cook dinner tonight."

He threw open the pantry doors. "Old Mother Hubbard went to the cupboard to get her poor dog a bone, but when she got there, the cupboard was bare—except for pet food. At least the animals will eat even if the people starve. Go get to work in your studio. I'm making the dessert for tonight."

When Natalie went to the kitchen to prepare dinner, there was no sign of a dessert. She molded the meat loaf into a heart shape, spooned tomato sauce over it and pierced it with a celery arrow. She put it in the oven with the two potatoes and a cabbage-in-cream-sauce casserole. She made a relish tray of raw carrots and pickles and olives.

She set the table in the living room with red place mats and white napkins and put her valentine in the center of the table and shook her head. It was garish, an enormous red heart studded with bits of lace, flowers cut from the remnants of wallpaper from her bedroom, a cat cut from a piece of calico, a dog from a piece of checked gingham, a picture of an embryo traced from a childbirthing book. At least she'd had the good sense not to include a sentimental verse.

She shrugged her shoulders and called Jack to dinner, clenching and unclenching her fists as he entered the living room, looked at the table and then picked up the valentine. He studied it and then he grinned.

"I never...it's...thank you, Natalie." He kissed her cheek. He was more eloquent in describing the meat loaf. "Clever, amusing, delicious."

When they had finished eating, he cleared

the table and then went upstairs to return with a cake, which he set in front of Natalie. The cake was lopsided and the icing was cracked, but stuck in the center of the cake were two little gold hearts.

"I'm sorry about the cake," he whispered. "I don't know what I did wrong. The picture in the cookbook was so pretty. I think maybe I cooked the icing too long..."

"Oh, Jack, I think it's lovely. If it were perfect, I'd think you bought it and I don't want a bakery cake. And these?" She lifted one of the gold hearts from the icing and removed a tiny piece of foil from its base. It was an earring. A pair of simple, gold earrings. "They're lovely." She swallowed the lump in her throat. "You couldn't have bought them recently. You thought about Valentine's Day way back..."

"Weeks ago." He pulled a flat paper bag from under the cake plate. "This is for Dodo," he said, removing a tiny undershirt printed with red hearts. "The lady at the shop assured me that babies are really this small when they're born. Do you believe that?"

"I believe that you are a dear, thoughtful man."

"Cut the cake," he said. "If you can chop your way through that icing."

When at last their lane had been plowed, Jack announced that he would drive to Pittsfield to replenish their larder. "No, Natalie, you may not go with me. I have no idea what the roads are like beyond our lane."

Neither did Natalie. She spent the afternoon sitting by the window, waiting. She tried to read, but the words on the page were replaced by pictures of the little car skidding on the ice, careening into a snowbank. By four o'clock she was pacing the floor, her breath coming in gasps, her hands sweating.

When at last she heard the car, she burst into tears and then dried them quickly and ran to open the door for him. He staggered into the kitchen with two huge bags of groceries, which he deposited on the table, and then went back for more.

"Good grief," Natalie exclaimed when he

returned from his third trip to the car. "You've bought groceries for an army."

"No, just for a blizzard. The winter is still young." He removed his down jacket and handed her a bag imprinted with the name of a Pittsfield bookstore. "This is what took me so long. I'm afraid you're never going to get to those childbirth classes so we'll just have to conduct our own."

The bag contained three paperback books about natural childbirth. After dinner that night, Jack studied them briefly and then coached Natalie through the first exercise. During the following week, they both read all three of the books.

When Babs stopped by one afternoon, they asked her to look through the books and mark the exercises she thought most useful.

She read them willingly. "You've got to learn to relax, to pant and to deep-breathe," she said, "but the most important thing is to have your husband right there with you all of the time."

Natalie did not tell Babs that she would be facing childbirth alone.

Natalie also discussed natural childbirth with Veronica. For the first time in their lives, the sisters had something to talk about that was equally interesting to both of them, and important, too. Veronica was enthusiastic about Dodo and offered to come when the baby was due. She sounded disappointed when Natalie said that she and Jack would manage by themselves.

In addition to the baby, the sisters discussed Veronica's graduate-level course entitled "Women Novelists in the Age of Victoria."

"I wish my husband and my mother were as interested in it as you are," Veronica said wistfully.

Celeste thought Veronica had been sent to college to find a husband. She'd done just that, so why would she want to return? Besides, Celeste liked to shop and lunch with her daughter and Veronica now insisted she had to stay home to study.

The doctor's attitude was "out of sight, out of mind." He didn't want to hear about her course—her professor was probably a dyke—and he certainly didn't want his comfortable life to change. So Veronica was juggling her time so that when he came home her books were out of sight and a three-course meal was ready to be served at the dining room table.

"I just hope he'll let me go on. I'd like to take two courses next semester."

"Are you going for your master's?" Natalie was amazed.

"I was thinking of getting a Ph.D.," Veronica whispered. "But Cedric will never..."

"So don't tell him. Just work away..."

Money, it turned out, was Veronica's problem. She would have to ask Cedric for the money for tuition and books.

"Take the money from your inheritance account."

"It's in Cedric's name. I thought...I know so little about investing. Besides, Cedric is very generous. He gives me anything I ask for, but this is different. He'll think I'm trying to compete with him."

Natalie offered to open an account in Veronica's name so that she could draw on it, for tuition and books. Veronica refused the gift; she eventually agreed to a loan—just until she was teaching and earning money herself.

One night Natalie told Jack about Veronica. "Beside producing a baby, this marriage has done something else for me," she said. "It has brought me close to my sister."

"You weren't close before?"

"Never."

"Why?"

"I guess I was jealous of her. She's the baby and beautiful and Mother is so proud of her."

"But you're the talented one." Jack sounded amazed. "Veronica is pretty in a conventional sort of way, but you...you're different. I expect she's a conventional sort of thinker, too. But I'm glad you feel close to your sister. I always regretted not having a sibling, even one to fight with."

"I always thought it would be nice to be an only child. Until now. Now I am very glad that I have a sister and that my sister is Veronica."

By the end of February the *Child's Garden of Verses* was completed.

"Let's have an art show," Jack said. "I'll set them all around the living room, gallery style."

"And invite Babs and Bob to come to see them. See if they can recognize their own children."

They set the paintings on tables and chairs and windowsills around the room. They put the one for "Dark brown is the river" on an easel. Jack was effusive in his praise.

"What happens to these when the book has been printed?" he asked.

"They'll be returned to me. Sometimes I sell illustrations that can stand alone. Sometimes I give them to a library. I'll give Babs the ones with her children in them."

"And I could buy the one with Copper and Silver in the living room?" Behind his glasses, Jack's little blue eyes danced.

"That's 'Summer Sun.' You may not buy it, but I will give it to you. I won't have it back for about a year, but you can collect it sometime when you come to visit Dodo...if you still want it."

"I'll want it." He stood in front of the picture. "I'll never want to forget that complacent cat. You've caught her just as I have seen her hundreds of times, sleeping with one eye open. As for Copper, he looks like he's ready to jump right out of the picture to lick your face. Do you think Copper is a typical dog or is he very special?"

"He's very special, at least to me."

Natalie was pleased with the pictures, too. As was usual for her, she spotted things she wished she had done differently. But all in all they were among the best she'd ever done and she knew it.

Babs and Bob were delighted with them and thrilled with the idea of owning paintings of their children. "Are you really going to give us all three of these?" Bob asked.

"If they are still intact after the book is printed. And these two little spot drawings."

"I hear you're a teacher," Bob said to Jack. "So am I. Teach history in Stockbridge. There'll be an opening for a math teacher next fall if you're interested."

Jack shrugged his shoulders.

It was a pleasant evening.

"I'm glad you have a friend like Babs," Jack

said as they were getting ready for bed that night.

"So am I." Natalie's mind was on her next problem. She stood beside the bed, biting her lower lip.

"Didn't you enjoy this evening?" Jack asked. "Was something wrong? You couldn't have expected *more* praise for your pictures."

Natalie laughed. "I loved this evening and I was *not* disappointed. It's just that I can't figure out how I am going to get the artwork crated and shipped to New York."

"You'd actually trust your pictures to the post office?"

"UPS."

"But what if they were lost or damaged? You have no duplicates."

"I'll insure them."

"And maybe have to do them all over again? That's absurd. You've worked months on them. Why risk losing them?"

Natalie looked down at her bulging stomach. "You think I could carry them on the train?"

"No, but I could take them in your car and I

will. I'll only be gone one day. Will that be all right? You could call Babs if you needed anything."

Natalie was amused. "You know, Jack, other husbands go to work every day and leave their pregnant wives at home."

"I am not other husbands. I am a *contract* husband. Or had you forgotten?"

She shook her head sadly; she'd *like* to forget.

A few days later Jack was up at dawn, loading the illustrations into Natalie's car. Early in the afternoon she received a phone call from her editor, whose response to the illustrations was more than Natalie could have hoped for. She loved them. The children had personality; the animals had character. Stevenson himself would have been delighted.

"And your husband, Natalie! What a treat to meet him. He's so proud of you and thrilled about the baby. Where did you ever find such a jewel?"

The answer on the tip of Natalie's tongue

was *I bought him*. Fortunately the editor went on with barely a pause:

"I'm sending a manuscript for a picture book along with him. He said you probably wouldn't feel up to working on it until after the baby arrives, but please read it and let me know if you want to do it on the usual split commission basis. The author will be content to wait to have her story illustrated by Natalie and I really think you may like it."

Jack arrived home in time for dinner. His face was etched with tired lines but he was smiling. "I wish I'd had a tape recorder with me, Natalie. They invited me into the editor's office while she and some other people looked over the illustrations."

"Who was there? The art director?"

"Yes. And a sort of beefy-looking woman who kept nodding and talking about how the librarians were going to love it."

"That's the woman in charge of library promotion."

"And a youngster with bright red curls

who giggled a lot. I'm glad I went. The only publishers I've met have been doing textbooks. They're a humorless lot. These ladies have the same kind of whimsical humor you have."

"My editor thinks you're a jewel. I agree. Thanks for making the delivery." She reached out to take his hand.

He pulled it back. "That's the good news; now for the bad. You can't drive that car anymore."

"Why? Did you have an accident?" Natalie was alarmed.

"No, but I'd be dead if I had. That tin can with wheels offers no protection. It's sluggish. It has no power when you need it. It steers like a lawn mower. I will not have you driving around in that thing with a baby. I'm going to buy you a suitable, full-size car."

"You are not. I like my car, but if you feel so strongly about a bigger car, I'll buy it myself."

"It will wipe out your bank account, unless you take out a loan."

"So it will wipe out my bank account. I'll be getting the second half of the advance on the

Stevenson in a few days and royalties are due this month. Don't worry, Jack. I can afford a car."

Jack selected and Natalie paid for a sedate Detroit sedan that had only two things to recommend it to Natalie. It was blue and there was room for the rapidly expanding mother-to-be behind the steering wheel. Jack insisted on buying a deluxe car seat with so much padding it was like a cocoon.

"You're sure you don't want me to put a helmet on Dodo whenever we go out?" Natalie laughed.

"Do you think they make infant-sized motorcycle helmets?"

Natalie wasn't sure if he was joking or not, but she couldn't help laughing at her mental picture of a tiny baby in a huge helmet. "Try not to be overprotective," she warned him.

He bristled. "I'm not overprotective. Dodo's safety is in your hands, not mine. I'm just doing what I can to see that this child reaches adulthood."

They stopped at a restaurant on the way home and Jack suggested that it was time to get the baby's room ready. He'd move his computer into one corner and they could do whatever had to be done to the back bedroom.

"Oh, no! The little room opposite the bathroom was meant for a nursery. I've never used it. I thought I'd just paper it and put the crib in there."

Jack smiled. "Okay. Let's go buy the paint and paper and I'll get to work on it right away. The weather might not hold and we'll be snowed in again. Better do it this afternoon."

Natalie sighed as he drove to a shopping center. He got out of the car, but she didn't move. He came around to her side of the car, opened her door and looked at her. "You're exhausted. Stay right there. I'll go buy white paint for the woodwork. You will want it white, won't you? We can get the wallpaper later."

"Buy white paint for the walls, too," she whispered.

Either Natalie slept or Jack was incredibly speedy because he was back almost as soon as he left. He parked the car close to the front door, helped her inside and upstairs.

"I'm sorry," he said. "I should have known how tired you'd be. It's been a long day."

When Jack had finished the tiny room, Natalie painted a huge cluster of balloons on the wall where the crib would be. On the other walls she scattered a few more balloons and flowers and one tiny kitten.

"Somehow I see a kite on the ceiling." She looked down at her huge bulk. "But maybe I'd better wait until after. I'm too awkward to go climbing around on a ladder. But maybe if you held it . . ."

"Nothing doing. I'll paint the kite."

So Natalie cut a stencil out of shelf paper and Jack taped it to the ceiling and filled in the color. They bought a changing table, a chest of drawers and a crib—all white—and unpacked the box Veronica had sent. The next time Jack went to the supermarket he came home with a huge box of disposable diapers. The room was ready and both parents were satisfied.

* * *

Natalie had enjoyed her pregnancy, even the early nausea and exhaustion. The middle period of good health and productivity had been a delight. During the last phase, she felt lethargic. She read a lot, and napped. She didn't have the energy to take the childbirth course. Still, it was a peaceful, contented time.

She had only one major problem. She couldn't see her feet, but she knew that her toenails needed clipping. One evening, after her shower, she made a determined effort to reach her toes. She tried to put one foot up on the bed. She could get it there, but there was no way she could maneuver so that she could see her toes. She tried sitting on the bed and drawing her foot up beside her. She turned this way and that, but still her girth was a barrier between her hands and her feet.

"Got a problem, lady?" Jack was standing in the doorway laughing.

"Yes, I've got a problem. I feel like a hippopotamus. Both in size and in beauty. Pregnant women are supposed to look like madonnas. I don't. I've never been pretty and now my face is splotchy and my hair is limp." She threw herself down and cried. She couldn't even get her body into the classic face-in-the-pillow position for crying, and that made her sob even louder.

Jack sat on the bed beside her and rubbed her back silently while she continued to cry. Then he stopped rubbing and took one of her feet in his hands and began to clip her toenails in his usual awkward but thorough manner. Natalie sat up against the pillow and watched him, tears still trickling down her nose. When he had finished, she drew him to her and kissed him.

"Oh, Jack, I do need you."

He pushed her back on the pillow and left the room. She heard his feet on the stairs. A few minutes later he was back thrusting a sketch pad and a selection of pencils at her, scowling.

"Draw yourself as a hippopotamus," he commanded. "And try to regain your sense of humor and perspective." He stormed into his computer room and she sat up and began to draw. In the morning the sketch was gone from her pad. She was feeling cheerful.

March days were unpredictable but generally warm. On the first day of spring it was so warm that they went for a long walk.

And then God pulled an April Fool's joke, the blizzard that Jack had stocked up for in February. Snow fell for two days. Winds raged.

On April 3, when the storm was over, Natalie set up her easel and painted the orchard through the small panes of the living room window.

She was putting the finishing dabs on the painting when she sensed Jack's presence behind her. She turned to him. He was smiling but he was not entirely pleased.

"So what do you think?" she asked.

"It's lovely."

"But?"

"I said it's lovely..."

"But?"

"I was thinking about Christmas. Remember how the tree sat right there beside the window? I just thought . . ."

Natalie picked up her brushes and painted in a few branches of pine at the right side of the window. Then she dotted it with tiny candle lights.

"Don't forget the cranberries and the popcorn," he said.

She added dots of red and white and looked at him again.

His smile was radiant. "What do you call it?" he asked.

Carefully she wrote at the bottom of the picture: "Lumpy Brides at Christmas."

He kissed the back of her neck and she felt herself tremble. "I hope you have a place for all these paintings," she said.

"I'll find a place." He all but ran to the back doorway, where she could hear him putting on his boots and heavy jacket. A few minutes later the door slammed and she caught a glimpse of him as he tramped into the woods with Copper running beside him.

Natalie sighed and patted her stomach. "Your father is a strange one," she said aloud.

"Anytime the atmosphere turns sentimental, he walks out. Had you noticed that?"

The snow melted quickly, leaving puddles and mud all over the yard. Natalie became even lazier. She drew only one more picture—after she had wondered aloud if her pregnancy would last forever.

"Probably," Jack said seriously. "You wanted to be pregnant and the man upstairs heard and answered. It isn't His fault that you weren't specific. You should have designated a time limit. But you didn't, so He probably thought you wanted to be pregnant forever. Too bad about that."

The picture showed a kangaroo with Natalie's weary face and a pouch so large that it seemed implanted in the ground. Inside the pouch was a boy kangaroo standing in the classic batting position. Off to the side, a slim kangaroo with black-rimmed glasses was preparing to pitch the ball to the boy. The mother kangaroo was going to be hit, either by the bat or by the ball.

"Poor mother kangaroo," Jack sympathized when he saw the picture.

"Poor boy kangaroo," said Natalie. "He doesn't have a name. How about John V. Berkhardt, Jr.?"

"Never." Jack's voice was sharp. "But the boy needs a name. What name do you like?"

"How about James? Jimmy? Jamie? Jim?"

"If you really like the name..." Jack was tentative.

"You don't."

"The bully at my boarding school was named James. A rotten kid."

"So it won't be James. You make a suggestion."

Jack was silent for a long time. "Do you like Andrew?" he said at last. "Andrew Carnegie. Andrew Mellon. He might grow up to be a philanthropist."

"Andrew. Andy. Drew..."

"Not Drew. Sounds like a movie actor or a playboy."

"Andrew. Fine. That's settled. So come on out, Alice or Andrew, and say hello to your parents." She looked up into a wistful smile. "Who

do you know named Andrew, beside the phi-
lanthropists?"

"My father," Jack whispered. "He was a
good man, Natalie. A grandson would have
meant a lot to him."

SPRING AGAIN

AS THE WEATHER GREW WARMER AND THE DAYS grew longer, Natalie became increasingly lazy. Her sleep was disturbed many times during the nights and she took long naps during the days. Still, Jack insisted that they continue the exercises outlined in the books. They went for long walks every day that it did not rain. Natalie began to look forward to rain.

And then one morning she awoke filled with energy. She hurried to the kitchen and began cleaning the refrigerator. By the time Jack came down for breakfast, she had emptied one of the cupboards and was relining the shelves.

He commanded her to stop, but as soon as he had returned to his computer room she filled a bucket with soapy water and got down on her hands and knees to scrub the kitchen floor.

Her maternity top trailed in the water, but she didn't care. The floor would be sparkling and then she'd start another project. She didn't hear the car in the lane. She didn't hear anything until the floor was finished and she was backed into the doorway, where Babs and Jack stood staring down at her.

"Good God," Jack swore. "I told you to stop."

"You told me to quit cleaning the cupboards. You didn't say a thing about the floor."

She wanted to stand, but she was so weighted that she couldn't get to her feet. She shifted her weight from her knees to her bottom and sat on the floor in the doorway. Without another word Jack came and planted himself in front of her and began pulling on her hands. Babs hoisted her under her arms. They led her to the couch.

Natalie laughed. "How undignified." Neither Jack nor Babs joined in her laughter.

"Does your back ache?" Babs asked.

"Come to think of it, it does. Way down low. Let's have coffee."

"I think I'll go home and let you rest," Babs said. "Happy birthing," she called back from the front door.

Jack walked Babs to her car and then came back and stood in front of Natalie. "I am very cross with you," he said, smiling, "but Babs assures me that you are exhibiting all of the symptoms of a lady about to go into labor. The book didn't mention a sudden spurt of energy."

"But Babs is an expert. She's spent three years being pregnant. Guess I'll just run upstairs and wash my hair on the outside chance that she is right." Natalie felt like leaping to her feet; her body felt otherwise. Jack took her hands to help her. "Soon I may not need a derrick every time I want to get up."

Jack followed her upstairs and when she had washed her hair he led her firmly to the bed, in spite of her protestations that she just wanted to do light work now, like cleaning the silver. She came downstairs for the lunch Jack had prepared, bouillon, of all things. She wanted a hamburger.

After lunch they walked up to the road, past the apple trees that were beginning to green.

"Maybe I should paint them once more. Just a watercolor sketch. What do you think?"

"I think you're either a fool or drunk. You didn't drink while you were scrubbing, did you, Natalie? You wouldn't." Jack was definitely not sharing her euphoria.

"I didn't. Come on, Jack, smile. This is a glorious day. I feel wonderful. Hungry but wonderful."

"How about your back?"

She stopped to consider. "Yes, it does hurt just a bit, actually a bit more than it hurt this morning."

At the road they turned back and by the time they reached the house Natalie was almost too tired to climb the stairs, a feeling she did not share with gloomy Jack.

She fell onto the bed and slept. She opened her eyes to see Jack staring at her from a chair he had placed by the side of the bed.

She still felt terrific. She swung her legs over the side of the bed and heaved herself to a standing position and waddled off toward the bathroom.

"Just call me ducky," she said.

Jack waited for her in the hall and escorted her back to the bedroom.

"Think I'll put on something pretty and then maybe you'll take me out to dinner," she said.

He pushed her to a sitting position on the bed. "Just sit there awhile."

"But I want to go out to dinner. Dancing, maybe." She looked down at her body and grimaced. "Maybe that's not such a good idea. How about a movie?"

"You don't feel anything?"

"A few twinges. Same as I've been having off and on for weeks. Perfectly normal, according to the doctor and the books."

"Your back?"

"It aches. Your back would, too, if you'd been carrying Dodo and a ton of water around for . . . oh . . . oh . . . oh . . . ?" She lay back against the pillow.

Jack watched her closely. "What did you just feel?"

"Pressure. It might have been an honest-to-goodness contraction. On the other hand, it might just have been an exaggerated twinge. Who knows? Why don't we just go downstairs and get some dinner—going out may not be such a good idea—and wait and see what develops."

"I've got a better idea. Why don't you stay where you are? I'll stay where I am, and we'll see what develops."

"Never. You're obviously some kind of a sadist intent on forcing me to starve to death, but I will not allow Copper and Silver to starve along with me." She spoke in mock severity.

"I'll feed them—a little thin gruel." He chuckled, but worry lines grooved his forehead. He ran down the stairs, calling the animals. He was back in what seemed to Natalie like ten seconds. "Did you feel anything while I was gone?"

"Boredom. Intense boredom. But now that you are here, you can entertain me. Tell me a joke."

"Come off it, Natalie. This is Jack here. Did you ever hear me tell a joke?"

"So start nooooooow." Startled, she grabbed his hand.

He looked at his watch, pulled an index card out of his pocket and recorded the time on it.

When the contraction subsided, she lay perfectly still for a moment and then she raised herself onto her elbow. "What's with the index card? You've got a computer. Why don't you feed the information into it? Computerized labor. Don't you think that's an innovative idea?"

"I do not."

"Maybe you're right. Two contractions do not a labor make. Still, you could be designing a program, or whatever you do, for when labor actually starts. If you're not going to tell me jokes, you might just as well get to work on it."

He scowled at her and then began to thumb through the book on childbirth that he had been studying for months. "Maybe you should walk."

"Good idea. Let's go look at the stream."

She did a very pregnant lady's version of jumping out of bed, and headed toward the stairs.

"Stop," Jack commanded. "You can look at the stream from the back room."

"The door is probably booby-trapped to keep me out. Besides, I can't smell the pines from the back room."

"I've had the mines removed. You're welcome to enter. And I'll open the window so you can smell the pines." He took her arm and led her through his immaculate room to the window, where they stood for a moment. "Now let's go look at the orchard," he said, leading her back the width of the house toward the window in their bedroom. She didn't make it to the window but gasped just inside the doorway. He led her to the bed, took out his card and picked up the telephone.

"Thirteen and a half minutes," she heard him say when she was able to hear anything. "She acts like she's on a high . . . That's normal? . . . Okay, we'll leave here when the contractions are eight minutes apart. You're sure that will give us enough time?"

"You didn't need to call the doctor yet," Natalie said. "Maybe in the morning."

Jack helped her to her feet and they walked to the window overlooking the orchard.

"Hey, you old brides, eat your hearts out. I'm going to have a baby. You may be impressed with those silly little red balls that you produce, but I'm not."

Jack groaned, but he didn't say anything.

An hour later it was dark outside. Jack's card had nine entries on it. Natalie was tired of walking.

"Okay," he said after the next contraction. "We're going to the hospital."

"The last two pains were more than eight minutes apart," Natalie said.

"Eight and half, to be precise."

"I'll be lonely in that big white hospital with no one to tell me jokes." She covered her mouth with her hand. "I'm sorry, Jack, I shouldn't have said that. Of course I can handle this by myself. If you want to turn me over to the nurses now, that's okay. You've been terrific this afternoon. I am grateful. Very grateful." Why, she asked herself, were her eyes feeling misty? She turned away from him and went to get her suitcase out of her closet.

Jack pulled into a "no standing" zone in front of the hospital, switched off the engine and jumped out of the car while Natalie was still struggling to open her door. He opened it and swung her legs around so that her feet were on the curb. Then he hoisted her out of the car to a standing position and started to walk her toward the hospital entrance.

"You can't leave the car here. Let's just say good-bye. I'll phone you as soon as I can. So long, Jack. I'm off to have a—"

"I'm coming with you."

"And get a ticket? That's dumb. You're treating me like an accident victim. Need I remind you that my condition is no accident?" Natalie laughed gleefully.

Jack continued to march her toward the door. A skinny old nurse who looked like an eagle rushed toward them, pushing a wheelchair. She motioned for Natalie to sit in it.

"I don't need a wheelchair." Natalie

laughed. "Ladies in labor are supposed to walk. It hurries things along. Besides, I feel terrific. I could climb a moun—"

Pressure—not pain, she had to remind herself—invaded her body so that she could not resist when the nurse and Jack lowered her into the chair. The nurse wheeled her off and the pressure receded.

"My insurance card," she called back to Jack. "It's here in my purse." She tugged at the nurse's sleeve. "Wait. My husband needs my insurance card."

"Go on," Jack shouted to the nurse. "I'll register her with my insurance."

"My insurance," Natalie insisted, but the eagle pushed her on into the elevator. "I wanted to use my insurance, not his."

"What difference could it possibly make?" The nurse sounded disgusted.

Before Natalie could explain how important it was, she was being pushed out of the elevator to be met by another nurse, stout and matronly-looking, who nodded to the eagle and took over.

"First baby?" the matron asked. "And you're how old?"

"Thirty-four." Natalie felt like giggling again. "A very young thirty-four. I fully expect to breeze through this. Remember, no drugs, no anesthesia. I want to experience every moment."

"Sure." The nurse sounded skeptical. "Your husband going to be with you?"

"No. He may be here for a few minutes. We didn't have a chance to say good-bye. On the other hand, maybe he'll just go on home."

"Good. I've been helping to deliver babies for almost thirty years now. It's women's work."

"My husband's good at women's work. He can cook and scrub and wash dishes..."

"Even Superman can't give birth."

Natalie, dressed in a hospital gown, was lying on the narrow bed. The nurse left the room. A contraction. She gave it her full attention, breathing deeply, then expelling all of the air in her lungs. And again. She fell back, lying rigidly.

"Sigh and relax," Jack shouted from the doorway. "Sigh and relax. Can't you hear me? I said sigh and relax. That's what you're supposed to do after the contraction. Where's the nurse?" Jack stood over her, frowning.

Natalie sighed and relaxed. "I'm glad you came up. The eagle whisked me away before we had a chance to say good-bye. Wish me luck, old Dad, and you can be on your way."

He responded by sitting on the bed, pushing her over onto her side and rubbing her back. "We'll be ready next time."

For the next hour Jack coached her through each contraction. The matron and a resident checked her from time to time. And then everything stopped and Natalie dozed. Through the haze she could hear Jack shouting at the nurse.

"It happens," the nurse said calmly, "especially with older first-time mothers. Nothing you or I can do about it. Just let her rest. Your first?" Jack must have nodded because the next words from the nurse were, "It figures. Old fathers are worse than old mothers."

"We're not old," Natalie muttered, "just mature."

Jack held her hand. He was still holding it when she woke again with the onslaught of pressure that was the worst pain Natalie had ever felt. Pain followed pain, closer and closer. She heard a cry and knew it came from her. She tried to concentrate on the exercises. Her doctor came in, examined her and smiled. The pain intensified. "I will not scream," Natalie said to herself, and then screamed.

"Breathe, dammit!" Jack shouted at her. "You think we spent all those hours doing exercises for the fun of it? Breathe properly. Hear me?"

Natalie was engulfed in pain. Jack stood over her, his hand raised as if to slap her. "Concentrate, Natalie, on breathing." He demonstrated and, at last, she focused on him and followed his instructions. The pain waned. Sweat was pouring down his cheeks. There were tears in his eyes.

"Why don't you wait outside?" she whispered, and then another pain invaded her body. When it was over she was still clinging to his hand. She released it and saw blood oozing from a scratch across his palm. "Did I do that to you?" She wanted to speak aloud but she could only whisper.

He wiped the blood on his pants and took her hand again. He held it as she was wheeled into the delivery room.

"You've been wonderful." She squeezed his hand. "But you don't have to stay with me now."

They lifted her onto a table and Jack appeared by her side dressed in a blue gown with a mask over his face. He pressed his cheek against hers. "I'll be sitting right behind you," he whispered. "I love you, Natalie."

Another pain. The doctor took over the coaching. "Bear down. Again. Harder. Pushhhhhh."

Her husband was sitting behind her, stroking her head. Nurses were at her side. Natalie was completely isolated, concentrating on the doctor's voice, her own body and the mirror in which she finally caught a glimpse of her baby's head. One more gargantuan push. The baby's head slid out into the doctor's hand, then the shoulders.

"A perfect little girl," the doctor said.

"Get that baby to her breast." It was Jack shouting. Jack. She'd forgotten all about him. She turned to try to find him, but he was no longer sitting behind her. The door swished open. "Welcome, Alice," he said softly. The door swished closed.

"I thought he'd want to hold the baby," the doctor said.

"It's been years since I've seen a man cry like that during delivery," someone said. "And I took him for a tough cookie."

The voices were far away. Natalie had her baby in her arms. "Welcome, Alice," she whispered as she examined the tiny creature and kissed her head. She had black hair, like Jack's.

Mother and daughter were wheeled into the recovery room, where the nurse took Alice away. "Just for a few minutes," she explained when Natalie began to protest. "Weigh her and measure her and make her look all pretty for her daddy."

Natalie sighed. "She's beautiful just as she is."

* * *

A few minutes later Jack entered the room. His face was gray with fatigue.

"Good work," he said, taking her hand in his.

"You, too. You need some sleep, Dad. You look very tired."

He just nodded and the nurse reappeared with a bundle wrapped in a pink receiving blanket. She handed the bundle to Jack, who stood staring down. Tears rose in his eyes. "Here." He sounded choked. Gently he laid the bundle in Natalie's arms. "You have what you wanted. Good-bye, Natalie. Thanks. Thanks for everything."

"You'll come see us tomorrow?"

"No. Veronica will be here. I can't stay." The door closed behind him.

In the delivery room Jack had told her that he loved her. Of course, he was overwrought, but still . . . She didn't know where he was going or for how long.

"He'll be back, Alice," she whispered, kissing her baby's downy black head. Then she unwrapped the child and examined her tiny toes and fingers, her little squished nose. She put the baby to her breast. Jack would be back. "Thank you, God," she murmured, "for sending me Jack and for this tiny miracle." Then she laughed. Tiny as Alice was, it seemed impossible to believe that she had come from Natalie's body.

After lunch the next day, Natalie put on a new nightie she had bought for the occasion and waited eagerly for visiting hours. Maybe Jack would have second thoughts. Maybe he'd be there.

At last there was the sound of footsteps in the hall and Veronica rushed through the door, beaming. Natalie looked beyond her. "Jack?" she asked.

Veronica pulled up a chair and sat beside her, taking her hand. "He phoned me. Said you needed me. He met me at the airport and drove me to your house and showed me how to drive your new car. He said he couldn't stay. No explanation. I don't understand this, Natalie, but I'm here for you and I'll stay as long as you need me."

"What about your children? And your Victorians?"

"There won't be any classes next week. Spring vacation. I brought a few of my Victorian novelists with me. As for the children, Mother's staying with them. You should have heard her when I said I was going to be with you. She wanted to come, but I was firm. Imagine that, I was firm with Mother! It took some doing, but I finally convinced her that my children needed her and you needed me."

"Have you seen Alice?" Natalie asked.

"She's beautiful. I can hardly wait to hold her."

"I forgot to ask how much she weighed." Natalie was chagrined at her own neglect. "How could I forget that?"

"You had other things on your mind. According to Jack, she weighed in at six pounds ten ounces and they rated her on a scale of ten —her breathing, her reflexes, her color, those kinds of things—and pronounced her a ten. She's a beautiful, perfect baby. I saw your doctor a few minutes ago and told her that your husband had to go away on business. I said I was here for you. She, the doctor, said that you breezed through delivery like a twenty-year-old."

"She calls that breezing? I don't think I could ever go through that again, not if my life depended on it."

Veronica laughed. "You feel that way now but wait a month. If mothers had to decide about second children during the first few days after the birth of the first, there would be no second children. Obviously they forget; look at all the second and third and fourth children in families. Speaking of which, your friend Babs said she'd be here this evening. Jack asked me to call her."

Three days later Veronica drove Natalie and Alice home and insisted that Natalie go straight up to her bed. Natalie didn't object; she wanted to get upstairs to see what of Jack's things he had taken with him. He had taken everything —his computer and everything that went with it. His section of the closet was empty, his drawers, even his shelf in the medicine cabinet.

Nowhere was there any trace of her husband. He had fulfilled his part of the bargain.

Natalie pulled off her clothes and climbed between the fresh sheets in her lonely bed and lay curled up in a ball. She tried to concentrate on Veronica's voice as she talked to the baby while she changed her diaper.

"That's a terrific nursery," Veronica said as she entered Natalie's room. Then she came and looked down at her, pushing her shoulder so that she could see into Natalie's face. "What is it? You look like you'd lost your last friend."

"I have." Natalie's body was racked with sobs and she couldn't control them; she didn't want to control them.

"Postpartum depression," Veronica said matter-of-factly. She sat on the bed beside Natalie, and the longer she sat the harder Natalie cried. At last Veronica went to the bathroom and came back with a glass of water.

"That's enough," she said sternly. "You'll make yourself sick and that will make Alice sick. I know that you have some problem with Jack, but this is not the time to wallow in self-pity. Pull yourself together, Nat." She took Natalie's shoulders and shook them. "I mean it. For Alice's sake you have got to get hold of yourself. Right this minute. Take deep breaths. Concentrate on them. Inhale. Hold it. Exhale. Hold it. Inhale..."

At last Natalie calmed and slept. When she awoke, Alice was demanding to be fed, and the simple act of nursing her baby calmed Natalie further.

During the next week Natalie felt like she was on an emotional merry-go-round. Up with the joy of this beautiful child whom she had carried in her womb, whom she could nourish from her own body, whose cries made her want to cry, whose sleep filled her with contentment. Down to the pits of loneliness. She had slept alone for thirty-four years, but her bed now felt empty. Alice was dark like her father; Natalie fancied that she scowled just like him.

When she had planned for a legitimate baby, she had not sufficiently considered the bond she would feel to the baby's father. Jack was still a stranger. She didn't know where he was. She didn't know who he was. He was as volatile as she had become during the last week.

The truth she finally acknowledged to herself was that she was in love with her baby's father. She hadn't planned for that. She had wanted to be a complete woman, to experience every joy and pain available to women. She had. She would never regret the ten months she had lived with Jack. He had taught her... But she was greedy; she wanted more.

She expected Jack to call, but he didn't. She thought about calling the answering machine, but he had probably disconnected it when his mother died. If she heard *That number is no longer in service*, it would seem final. She decided not to call.

One evening when Alice was two weeks old, Natalie and Veronica were sitting silently in the living room, Veronica doing needlepoint, Natalie doing nothing.

"Remember the afternoon you brought us home from the hospital?" Natalie said at last. "Boy, were you stern with me! I didn't know you had it in you. I needed just what you gave me. Thank you. Thank you for everything."

Veronica beamed. "I'm glad you're not angry. I haven't had a lot of practice in the standing-firm department, but I'm learning. The first time I tried to stand firm with Cedric, he was so angry I almost backed down. But I didn't." Veronica thrust her chin forward. "And he's beginning to come around."

"Have you told him about your Ph.D.?" Natalie asked.

"Not yet. That's far in the future. Just before I left, I gave him a choice: I could take two courses in the fall or one course during the summer and another in the fall."

"And?"

"He chose the two courses in the fall, so I'd be home with the children this summer. That's fine with me; I don't want to make too many changes in my life. I love Cedric and the children and I like to play tennis and entertain. I even like to shop and lunch with Mother if I don't have to do it every week."

"You are one interesting woman, Veronica." Natalie smiled at her sister. "And now it's time for you to go home. I'll find someone to drive you to the airport this weekend."

Veronica was silent for a moment. "I know you are hurting, Nat. If it would help you to tell me about it, you could. You could depend on me to keep your secret."

"I know that, Veronica, but . . ."

"And I wouldn't judge."

It would be a relief to tell someone, Natalie thought. At last she spoke.

"I wanted a legitimate baby and I paid Jack to marry me and try to impregnate me . . ."

"You what? Paid? You paid Jack?" Veronica clapped her hand over her mouth. "I just said I would not judge. I won't. So, you paid Jack to impregnate you . . ."

"Ten thousand dollars down and I owe him another ten thousand. I don't even know where to send it."

Veronica shook her head, bewildered. "You two seemed so happy together. He was so attentive and he gave you such lovely jewels. Maybe the payment you owe has something to do with the bankbook. You did see it, didn't you? I found it on the kitchen table and I put it in the top drawer of your desk. Maybe you haven't seen it." Veronica dumped her needle-point and ran to the studio, returning to hand Natalie a bankbook.

Natalie opened it and noticed that it was for a bank money fund. "Natalie Jones Berkhardt in trust for Alice Berkhardt, minor," she read aloud. There was one entry, for ten thousand dollars. "Why did he do that? We had a contract and everything. He earned his money. He didn't even deduct for the honeymoon expenses and the chain saw he used to trim the apple trees. Or for what I owe him for painting the shed..."

Veronica laughed. "Maybe he enjoyed impregnating you. Did you ever think of that? I can't believe he needs money. Look at the car he drives. Look at the suit he wore to the wedding. That didn't come off the rack. What do you know about your husband? Anything at all?"

Once Natalie started to talk, she couldn't stop. The baby cried. Natalie went upstairs to get her and brought her back. Natalie kept right on talking while she nursed Alice. Then she laid her on the couch. She told Veronica everything.

About how he made her body come alive so that she tried to suppress the first signs of pregnancy. How he had gone away and come back for the winter. About the huge Thanksgiving turkey and the train at Christmas. She even told Veronica about how he had cut her toenails.

"It seems perfectly obvious that he loves you," Veronica said at last. "Did he ever say he did?"

"Once. In the delivery room. But he was overwrought then. That didn't mean anything."

"Did you ever tell him that you love him?"

Natalie shook her head. "It was a simple business deal at first and then when he came back in the fall we became friends, very good friends. That's all either of us wanted. Thank goodness I didn't know then that I loved him; it would have made us so awkward with one another." Natalie laughed down at Alice. "He was such a dear friend, the best friend I ever had."

"So why don't you invite him to come for a visit, tell him you love him, see how he reponds?"

"You still don't understand, Veronica. I

don't know where Jack is. I don't even know who he is."

Veronica sat silently. "There's one question . . . Could he be a bigamist?"

Natalie shook her head. "I don't honestly believe that he ever lied to me except by implication. I asked him if he was married and he said he wasn't and that he never had been. I know he has had experience with women . . ." Natalie's cheeks grew hot. "But he may have been in jail. That's what I thought when I first met him. His skin was so pasty, like he'd been inside for a long time. Prison or a mental institution. But . . ."

"Now, you don't believe that." Veronica was so matter-of-fact. She got up and returned with a yellow legal pad and a pencil. "So let's write down what you do know about him. How old is he?"

"Thirty-eight. That's what he said."

"What's his profession? Was he really a high school math teacher?"

Natalie shook her head and told her sister about the encounter with the young man at

Tanglewood. "He called him 'Doctor' and 'Professor.' "

"Good. Jack's a college professor. What else?"

Natalie shook her head again and then she remembered his comments about textbook publishers after he had been to visit her publisher.

"Duck soup," laughed Veronica. "If he's the author of a textbook you should be able to trace him. The Jones Sisters, tracers of missing persons. That's us. You think his field is math?"

"Or some related field. He might be an accountant. He was a whiz with my taxes."

"We're making progress, old sis," Veronica exclaimed. "Now, what kind of college would he have taught in? Where? Why did he leave?"

Natalie said that he was raised in the Boston area and that the area code on his answering machine was eastern Massachusetts.

Veronica was silent. "What do you think of Harvard?"

"What should I think of Harvard? It's a fine institution."

"Oh, Nat." Veronica was disgusted. "Did Jack ever say anything that would lead you to believe that he might be on the Harvard faculty or have attended Harvard? If he went there you'd have to know it. Two of the doctors at the hospital went to Harvard Medical School and one of them went to Harvard as an undergraduate. Believe me, you can't be in their company for ten minutes without Harvard being dragged into the conversation. Harvard men make sure you know they went to Harvard. Cedric says it's endemic to the breed. He's jealous, you know, but he's right."

"Jack doesn't brag."

"So maybe he's the exception to the rule. Why don't you phone Harvard tomorrow and ask to speak to him? You can say you are his cousin, in town for a few days, and you want to make contact with him for old times' sake. If they've never heard of him, you can phone the next college you can think of in the area. It's time for bed, my dear Watson." Veronica let Copper out and when he returned she locked up the house, picked up the baby and went upstairs.

Natalie followed. In the upstairs hall she turned to her sister. "Thanks, Veronica," she said. "I will call Harvard but not now. Jack may still come back on his own. According to the contract, he has a right to see Alice twice a year. He'll want to see her. I'll know better what to do when I have seen him again. When we've settled down and can be unemotional."

"Frankly, I doubt that you'll ever be unemotional where he is concerned, but so be it. I'd be willing to bet big money on his love for you..."

"Not me, but maybe Alice. He's tormented by something. Do you think he could have stolen money from Harvard... or faked research ... or..."

Veronica patted her shoulder. "You are far too imaginative. So far what you've said suggests that he had a cold mother and a strange childhood. He probably just doesn't know much about loving or about demonstrating his love. You could teach him a lot, Nat. Perhaps you already have."

Three days later Babs drove Veronica to the airport, leaving Natalie in full charge of her baby for the first time. Babs checked in with her every day during the next two weeks, carefully avoiding any mention of Jack.

Natalie was anxious to fill every moment of every day. When Alice was four weeks old, she began work on the illustrations for the new picture book.

One morning that week, when Alice had finished nursing, she looked up at her mother and smiled for the first time. "Enchanting," Natalie breathed as she hugged her little warm baby to her. Then she laid her on the couch and ran for her sketch pad. She sketched in the baby's head and features and then she cooed and talked at her until suddenly Alice smiled again. Natalie sketched in the smile and sat back. Many times during the past four weeks she had been amazed at the depth of her love for this tiny creature. She had read about mother love; and now she was experiencing it. She was glad to have paid the price—even the pain of her separation from Jack—for this experience.

"We have got to find your father's address and share this smile with him," she said. "He's missing so much. He didn't know how much you would change from day to day when he wrote his dumb agreement."

The next morning Natalie lifted the phone with trembling hands and dialed information in eastern Massachusetts. Then she dialed the general offices number of Harvard and asked to speak to Dr. John V. Berkhardt.

"I don't have him listed. What department is he in?" the phone operator asked.

"Math."

The phone rang again and a man answered. "Harvard Math."

Again Natalie asked for Dr. Berkhardt.

"Don't I wish he were here," was the laughing answer. "But he's dyed-in-the-wool M.I.T. At least he was there until the scandal. Heard he left right after that newspaper piece. Call M.I.T. If he's not there, they'll know where to find him."

Natalie said thank you and hung up. For an hour she sat beside the phone staring out of the window, seeing nothing. Jack was an M.I.T. professor who had done something scandalous. Something of which he was so ashamed that he did not want a son named after him. Something that had caused him to ride off on a bike. She had no right to pry further. It was his secret.

Another two weeks passed and then Natalie left Alice with Babs for the first time while she drove to Pittsfield to the Berkshire Atheneum. First she looked at the card catalogue under "Berkhardt." Nothing. Then *Books in Print*. Nothing. She checked and saw that the volume did not include textbooks. Then—she could not stop herself—the microfilms of the Boston paper, searching backward from the day Jack arrived in her lane. She did not have to look long:

The headline read: "M.I.T. Professor Implicated in Suicide of Student." Natalie caught her breath and read on:

Shock waves raged through the M.I.T. campus yesterday following the discovery of the body of Anthony Caprella, a 19-year-old graduate student from New York City. Caprella, considered by many on the staff to be a prodigy of unusual promise, apparently hung himself in his dormitory room following a vicious verbal attack by Dr. John V. Berkhardt.

Berkhardt, himself a former prodigy, has done pioneer work in the development of computers for use by NASA.

A faculty member, who asked not to be identified, said that Berkhardt, age 38, had received his first degree from M.I.T. at the age of 18 and had earned Ph.D.'s in math and physics the following year. He has been a full professor for 11 years. The faculty member said that many mathematicians suffer "burnout" and that this had apparently happened to Berkhardt. Although he has made no major contributions to his field in recent years, he wrote a widely used, graduate-level text and continues to teach.

One of Berkhardt's students, who also asked not to be identified, said that the professor was highly respected if not loved. He said that the professor had been interested in Caprella's work and had encouraged him but that in recent weeks the young man had apparently been neglecting his work. During the last seminar before the student's death, Berkhardt had attacked him viciously in front of other students, calling him "lazy" and "irresponsible."

Dr. Berkhardt was not available for comment.

Anthony Caprella, a graduate of the Bronx

High School of Science, had received a full scholarship. . . .

Natalie had no recollection of leaving the library. She forgot to stop at the supermarket. Somehow she got to Babs' house, where Alice was howling with hunger. She nursed the baby and thanked Babs. As she was strapping Alice into the car seat, Babs came and stood beside her.

"Something is wrong," she said. "Can I help you in any way?"

"Nothing is wrong except in my head, Babs. I've just discovered a piece of information that I haven't had a chance to digest."

That night Natalie spent the evening curled up in the wing chair trying to sort out her thoughts. For the first time, Jack's character came into focus. He had an unloving childhood, but he had been a prodigy, and because he was so bright he was apt to be impatient with others. He was impatient with her. If he thought he was losing his creative powers, he would certainly be impatient with himself. He had lashed out—and she knew how he could lash out—at a favorite student and that boy had committed suicide. Poor, dear Jack! Carrying his guilt off on a bicycle. Painting her shed. Was it busywork or penance? Agreeing to father a child who might, in some mystical way, redeem a life.

He'd come away with a copy of *The Scarlet Letter*. A book about adultery? No, a book about guilt and atonement. She searched out a copy and read it far into the night.

The question that remained unresolved was how he felt about Alice. Was he disappointed because Alice was not a boy? Jack was not a male chauvinist. Still, he might have hoped to father another mathematical genius. Had there ever been a female math prodigy?

Her own relationship with Jack—from Jack's point of view—also came into focus. She was the vehicle through which he could produce the atoning child. Of course he would do everything possible to produce a healthy child by taking care of the mother. Of course he would love her in the moment that she was giving birth. He would not accept money, because he needed the child, too. He needed the child so much that he was willing to pay for it with expensive gifts. Natalie had sometimes thought that he might love her, for herself alone. How stupid of her! No man had ever loved her. Why should Jack be different from other men?

Did he still want a boy? They had not been unhappy together. Would he consider coming back to try again? So many questions. Only one certainty. Jack was in pain. She couldn't relieve his suffering, but perhaps Alice could.

Natalie had a long talk with Alice while she nursed her the next morning: "Your father needs you, my dear. He's hurting. He may have wanted a boy, but girls have a special bond with their fathers. You could bring joy back into his life—or maybe bring joy into his life for the first time. Keep your eyes open and concentrate on what I am saying, Alice. It's important. We'll begin by sending him the sketch of your smile. I'll mail it to M.I.T. marked 'personal, please forward.' That might bring him back. What do you think?"

Alice kept her thoughts to herself.

Mother and daughter took the sketch, carefully shielded in a mailing bag, to the post office. The postmistress had a Boston phone book. Without hope, Natalie asked to see it, turned quickly to Berkhardt, and there he was for all the world to see. J. V. Berkhardt lived in Cambridge. Natalie crossed out the M.I.T. address and wrote in the one in the phone book. She wrote the address a second time on a slip of paper and dropped it in her purse. Then she mailed the picture and went home to wait for Jack's response.

The apple trees were beginning to bloom. Surely Jack wouldn't miss his brides in their finery!

She worked most of the day in the yard, clearing the flower beds where peony bushes were poking through the ground, mowing the lawn. Copper helped her. Alice and Silver slept in the sun.

The next day Natalie was too restless to do anything. She scrubbed the kitchen floor, jumping up every time she heard a car on the main highway. She vacuumed and stopped before she was finished, and went outside, where she raked a few dead leaves and came back inside to be near the phone.

Her behavior was ridiculous, she told herself. The picture *might* be delivered that day; most likely it would not. If it did arrive, Jack might or might not be home to receive it. If he did receive it, he might not care anymore. "So that's Alice," he might say. "Nice-looking kid." Then he might just cast the sketch aside and go on with whatever he was doing. He could even have found another woman by now—it had been six weeks. So forget it, Natalie told herself. What will be, will be. Good advice, which she could not heed.

Deep within herself, Natalie cherished the hope that Jack would come back to live with them on a part-time basis. He would love Alice and that would bind them together. Natalie could not expect him to love her, Natalie, passionately. It would be enough if they could live together companionably, whenever he was free, as they had lived during the winter. Natalie was ready to accept any crumb, and ashamed because it was so.

* * *

She slept poorly that night. Alice whimpered at five-thirty the next morning and Natalie jumped out of bed to go to her. While she nursed, she made a sudden, irrational decision. She could not tolerate one more day of suspense. She had to have it out with Jack. If he didn't want them, he could tell her so to her face, and she would come back and make the best life she could for herself and Alice. And if he did want them . . . He could come in time to see his brides in bloom.

An hour later she had downed her coffee, packed a lunch and was driving down the lane. Copper bid them a loud farewell, running after them to the road and returning to guard the house. Silver slept on the porch railing. Alice was asleep in her car seat by the time Natalie turned the car onto the Massachusetts Turnpike.

Two and a half hours later, just outside of Cambridge, she stopped for gas and nursed Alice and put her in a pink smocked dress with matching panties.

"Lovely." Natalie cuddled her baby. "Your father will have to be captivated when he sees you in that dress. It brings out the rosy quality in your skin. You feel so soft and you smell so good. Just don't forget to smile. You do that better than anything."

Alice smiled.

The gas station attendant had never heard of the street she was seeking, but he brought out a city map. It was a tiny street just two blocks long, between Harvard and M.I.T., not far from Memorial Drive and the Charles River.

Crews were rowing on the river. The spires of Harvard rose above the trees. The traffic—it was just after rush hour—was overwhelming. But Natalie found the street of old clapboard houses and the number on a three-story mustard-colored house. Did Jack own the house? Hardly. But how could she know?

That there was a parking place right in front of the house seemed to her to be a good omen, but her heart was thudding in her chest and her knees felt quaky. She sat a moment trying to force a normal breathing pattern. And then she prayed. "Dear God, let him be there.

Let me say the right thing so that I won't make him angry. Help Alice to woo him. And...O God, I want that man."

Clutching Alice to her, she went up on the front stoop and rang the single bell. "What will I say to whoever answers?" she asked herself, and almost turned and ran back to the car.

She needn't have worried about what to say. A stout gray-haired woman in a crisp housedress opened the door a crack, then threw it wide. "Why, it's Mrs. Berkhardt and Alice," she said. "Come in, my dears. I've been dying to meet you. But..." She stopped. "What are you doing here? I thought the professor had gone to see you. He showed me the little cherub's picture yesterday and when I heard his car early this morning I thought...never mind. Maybe he just went to his office. You could call him there. In the meantime, I have a key and you can wait in his apartment. He's my favorite tenant. Should be. He's been with me longer than any of the others. Oh, you are precious!" She tickled Alice under the chin and was rewarded with a smile.

Then she went through a doorway off the

side hall and came back with a huge ring of keys and led the way up the stairs, stopping at the top of the first flight to open one of two doors. "I hope you'll like it," she said. "Anything you want, just let me know. I'd like to care for the baby if you want to go out. I'm really good with babies...I expect you know that. I expect the professor has told you everything there is to tell about me." She laughed heartily and then turned and went down the stairs.

"Thank you," Natalie called after her as she pushed open the door and stepped inside a narrow hall and switched on the light.

To the right was a small bedroom. She laid Alice in the middle of the bed, looked up at the wall beyond the side of the bed and gasped. Taped to it were dozens of snapshots and sketches—all of them by or of Natalie. There was the kangaroo with the boy in the pouch. Snapshots taken at the wedding and in Maine. One of Natalie in her first maternity dress.

There was also a perfectly dreadful picture which Natalie had never seen before. It had obviously been taken in her last month of pregnancy and she looked like a beached whale. She reached up to tear it from the wall and then thrust her hand behind her back. Was it possible that Jack liked that picture? On the tall chest was a studio portrait of a man who had to be Jack's father and the framed sketch of the angry bear scolding the pregnant rabbit.

Holding her breath, she crept out into the little hall. Opposite the bedroom was a bathroom with a tub on legs. Beyond was a small kitchen. The photograph of their Thanksgiving table was taped up above Jack's tiny table.

At the end of the hall was a huge book-lined room dominated by an enormous desk. Above the desk was the garish valentine, in an ornate gilt frame which was absolutely perfect for it. Over the fireplace were the three paintings of the orchard and a blank space for the fourth that was never painted. I'll do it this summer with Alice in the foreground, Natalie thought.

She dropped into his desk chair. It smelled like him and soothed her tense muscles. Lying squarely in the center of the blotter was the sketch of smiling Alice. Stuck into a corner of the blotter was a picture of Natalie cut from the jacket of one of her books.

She dared not think about the significance of all these pictures in his apartment. They could mean anything. Maybe he just wanted to remind himself constantly of how foolish he had been. On the other hand . . . There was a phone on the desk. She dialed a number she knew, her own. Off in the Berkshires, the phone rang twice and then a male voice said, "Hello."

"Hello, Jack."

"Where the hell are you?"

"Sitting at your desk in Cambridge. Alice is asleep on your bed. What do you think of the blushing brides?"

"What? If you're talking about the orchard, I haven't seen it. I got here ten minutes ago and your car was gone. What, in the name of Sam Hill, are you doing in Cambridge?"

"Alice wanted to meet her father. I drove her."

"Stop being whimsical. I came here so we could talk."

"So I'll come home."

"You will not. You will stay right where you are. Hear me?"

"Of course I hear you; you're shouting at me."

He paused. "Sorry. Please stay there, Natalie. I'll start back immediately. I . . ." He hung up.

Feeling like a spy, Natalie searched Jack's bookshelves for clues to her husband's character. Everything was neatly arranged. All of the math books—there were rows of them. She selected one, opened it, shuddered and put it back. Natalie had passed high school algebra by memorizing, not by understanding. She could never hope to converse with Jack about his field of interest. She went on to a row of books about investing. There were biographies of musicians and shelves of recordings of classical music. There was a complete set of the works of Nathaniel Hawthorne and beside it the biography she had given him for Christmas. And there were a dozen children's books, all of them illustrated by Natalie.

She also found the textbook by John V.

Berkhardt, Ph.D. It might have been written in Sanskrit, but the biographical information about the author was interesting. Dr. John V. Berkhardt, who received a Ph.D. in mathematics from M.I.T. at the age of nineteen, and one in physics at the age of twenty, had taught briefly at the University of California, Berkeley, before returning to M.I.T. where he was a full professor. He had made an important contribution to the space program.

Natalie heard the baby gurgle and went to pick her up. "Boy, do I know how to pick a father," she said to Alice. "For my sake, I hope you haven't inherited his brains. I wouldn't know how to cope with genius."

The baby spoke in her own language.

Natalie carried her down to the car to get the lunch she had packed. She ate it at the tiny table in Jack's kitchen. Then she changed the baby and lay totally relaxed on the couch to nurse her.

"I'll put the other dress on you and put a new face on me before your daddy gets here," she promised the baby.

* * *

Natalie did not keep her promise. The first thing she saw when she awoke was Jack's face. He was sitting on the floor so that his face was about six inches from hers. They simply stared at one another for a long time, then Natalie stretched and sat up.

"Good grief," she said. "I promised Alice we'd be all prettied up before you got here, and look at us!"

"Skip it." His eyes had turned cold. "I have something I want to say. Something I've driven all the way across the state and back again in one morning to say. You just sit there and listen. I don't want Alice to be an only child. I was one and you can see what kind of person I turned out to be."

"Terrible." Natalie giggled.

"Would you please refrain from frivolous comments until I am finished? Your doctor told me that she usually advises young mothers to wait several years to have a second child, but since you are not a young mother she suggested that if you wanted another child you shouldn't wait too long. Now, obviously, we are good baby makers."

Natalie giggled.

Jack frowned and then his face softened. "Funny thing happened in the delivery room," he mused. "I've often wondered if you felt it. We'd been talking about Dodo for months, but Dodo was like the character in a story, amusing but not quite real. And then this person, this real, live person entered the world. It wasn't Dodo, the storybook character, but Alice, another human being."

"I know," Natalie said simply.

Jack rubbed the back of his neck as if it were stiff. Then he took a deep breath. "Here's what I propose. I'm going to be teaching again this fall, but..."

"I'm glad to hear that, Jack."

"I could move in again this summer and we could try to make another baby. We might not be as speedy a second time. That may just have been luck. But I could come back weekends and vacations..."

"You really want a boy, don't you?"

He stared at her. "I don't care one way or

the other. I'd actually thought of another girl. You and Veronica are so close. That's good. Look, Natalie, I know you don't love me..."

"You're sure of that?"

"Come off it! We were—I hope we still are —very, very good friends. I've sometimes hoped that it could be more. But in the delivery room I was an emotional wreck and you didn't know I was there."

"I was busy."

"I told you I loved you and you didn't even hear me. You wanted a stud and that's what you got."

"I heard you. Do you love me, Jack?"

"What do you think?" Jack jumped up and strode toward the door.

Natalie picked up Alice and ran after him. "Come back here," she shouted. "I don't know what to think. If you can't tell me directly, take your baby in your arms and tell her what you think of her mother."

He looked at her in disbelief. Then he took Alice in his arms and came back and sat in his desk chair. Natalie sat behind them on the edge of the couch.

"I don't know much about babies, Alice, but I think you are beautiful." He smoothed her wrinkled dress. "I hope you'll grow up to look like your mother. You don't have a standard for comparison, but let me tell you this: Lots of women look attractive once they've put goo all over their faces and done silly things with their hair. Your mother wakes up in the morning pretty. Her eyes shine. Her hair is soft and glossy. And she has a compact little body. Even pregnant she looks well put together. She is kind and amusing. A good person, I'd say. But she has one terrible fault which I hope you will not inherit."

Natalie, who had been listening to his words with joy, felt her heart constrict.

"She keeps terrible records and I don't honestly believe she could add six two-digit numbers without the aid of a calculator. However, that's not important. What is important is your mother's work. Do you know that she enriches children's lives? She has enriched my life. The months I spent with her were the happiest months of my life, and making you was one hell of a lot of fun."

Alice began to cry and Natalie grabbed her and put her to her breast to quiet her.

He stood up and turned toward her, watching the baby nurse. "Beautiful," he whispered, and then turned away. "I shouldn't watch you do that, should I? Sorry."

"Why shouldn't you watch if you want to? Look, Jack, we've been through a lot together. You know everything about me."

"But you don't know everything about me. I've got to tell you something." His back was still turned to her.

"You don't need to; I already know."

"How could you know?"

"I read the Boston paper. I also reread *The Scarlet Letter*. You may have been thoughtless, even brutal, but you did not commit a sin. There had to have been other factors that led to the boy's suicide. Regardless of what the paper says, you alone were not responsible. You can't bring the boy back, but you can be there for other students . . ."

"Do you know why he was not doing good work? Because he had met a girl. He was in love with her and neglecting his work. I didn't un-

derstand how anything could be more important than his work. He was brilliant, capable of
creative thought. Now I understand and it is too
late. I would give up my whole career to have
met you before..."

"But you have met me now. What you
don't seem to realize is that I love you, Jack. I
have loved you for a long time, although I
didn't acknowledge my love, even to myself."
She laid the baby on the couch and went to
stand in front of him, standing silently until he
looked into her eyes. "I tried to hide my pregnancy so that you would stay with me longer.
This winter was the most beautiful season of my
life. I want you to come back to make another
baby. I'll settle for that if necessary. But I'd
choose, if I had the choice, to grow old with
you."

"You'd let me come every summer, every
weekend, every holiday?"

"I'd move in here if you'd take down those
pictures in your bedroom, especially the one of
me looking like a whale..."

He looked around his apartment, stunned.
"There isn't room..."

"It's all right, Jack. You can come whenever you want . . ."

"So we'll have to find a winter house. With a studio for you. You'd really come live with me? Forever?"

She nodded, unable to speak.

"I have loved you, Natalie, since the night of the lightning storm, and every day I have loved you more. Even when I was being the most disagreeable, I wanted to tell you I loved you. Maybe I'll be less bearish now that I can say what I want to say." He grinned. "But I wouldn't count on it."

Alice gurgled and Jack picked her up awkwardly and put her on his shoulder, holding her back with one hand. He scooped Natalie to him with his other arm and kissed her until Alice began to whimper.

"Hush," he said to Alice. "Your mother and I are busy."

Natalie did not paint the orchard that summer. She and Jack had to say all of the things they had not said in the past year. They had to find a winter house and furnish it. She had her work and he had his.

It was not until the following summer that she got around to painting the fruitful brides with Alice in the foreground. In the background a smiling bear with black-rimmed glasses held a very pregnant little brown rabbit between his paws.

By the author of the runaway
New York Times bestseller
The Shell Seekers

ROSAMUNDE
PILCHER

"I don't know where Rosamunde Pilcher has been
all my life—but now that I've found her, I'm not
going to let her go."
—*The New York Times Book Review*